DIRTY
COPPER

Library of Congress Cataloging-in-Publication Data

Northrup, Jim, 1943-
   Dirty Copper / Jim Northrup.
      pages cm
   Summary: "Dirty Copper, the prequel to Walking the Rez Road, tells the story of Luke Warmwater, an Anishinaabe soldier, as he returns to the Reservation after serving in Vietnam. Once again, Luke is torn between duty and morality as he becomes a deputy sheriff on the Rez and sees firsthand the war raging below the appearance of peace. Like all veterans, Luke struggles to heal amid a world that considers him an outsider. Jim Northrup provides an insightful and unflinching view of the veteran experience both as a soldier and as a Native American"-- Provided by publisher.

   ISBN 978-1-55591-864-4 (paperback)

   1. Vietnam War, 1961-1975--Veterans--Fiction. 2. Indian reservations--Fiction. 3. Ojibwa Indians--Fiction. I. Title.
   PS3564.O765D57 2014
   813'.54--dc23
                                    2014015076

Printed in the United States of America
0 9 8 7 6 5 4 3 2 1

Fulcrum Publishing
4690 Table Mountain Dr., Ste. 100
Golden, CO 80403
800-992-2908 • 303-277-1623
www.fulcrumbooks.com

DIRTY
COPPER

by Jim Northrup

FULCRUM PUBLISHING

Introducing... *Dirty Copper*

What is "dirty copper"? It could be *wiinagad miskwabik*, a dirty alloy, or *dakoniweininiish*, a questionable cop, or it could be the name young relatives give you when you show up back home dressed as an officer of the law. Jim Northrup's new novel, *Dirty Copper*, explores what that uniform means to a young Marine making sense of life back home. Whether he is charming women with his "*boozhoo*" and "welcome to Sawyer" or riding shotgun (literally) in a Carlton County cop car, Luke Warmwater is the same character readers remember from *Walking the Rez Road*. In *Dirty Copper*, he has more depth and detail. The stories are still sometimes funny, but in this longer novel of Luke's life and adventures, they are also sometimes sad. We can see a gentle side of Luke as he learns how much to keep to himself and how much to share with others as he makes sense of postwar life. We also witness the internal struggles that take place when one day Dad asks you to change the way cops treat your Anishinaabe relatives, and the next day he raises hell at the local bar. How does one man keep the peace: between Ma and Dad; between nightmares and reality; between the difficult past, the cautious present, and dreams of the future?

In his novel, Northrup wraps words around what comes after war, after loss, after pain and after grieving ... when life goes on. Although he writes the story in English it is a story of what is called in Anishinaabemowin, "*zaagi*," a word that is sometimes translated as "love" but means opening up, moving forward, connecting with life itself. These connections and the question of how to "survive the peace" trace back to one of Jim's early poems, "Shrinking Away," where the Vietnam veteran experience is revealed as extraordinarily complex and not something society was prepared to address. Consider the fact that the indigenous people of Vietnam were fighting to be free from colonial control, lived in round handmade homes with roofs thatched the way wigwams are fringed, centered their seasons on rice, and then consider how difficult it would be to serve a nation destroying a people and a culture that looked very much like one under quiet, continual siege back home.

I still remember the images of Mai Lai, and a little girl my age facedown in a pile of dead relatives, and, for me, that image was filtered by distance and a TV screen. Imagine looking war in the face every day. Although the world teaches us to see war from a distance, *Dirty Copper* teaches us not to look away when others struggle to "survive the peace." This novel shows us how much strength it takes to own your actions, to face reality, and to dare say, "Fuck it, I'm going home."

Margaret Noodin
Assistant Professor
English and American Indian Studies
University of Wisconsin–Milwaukee

CONTENTS

Part One.. 9

Part Two 101

Part Three 189

PART ONE

CHAPTER ONE

This was going to be a bad one, Luke thought in the first seconds of the ambush. The Marines were in a rice paddy, knee-deep water, ankle-deep mud. The VC were in the tree line about seventy-five meters away, shooting.

The point man of the fifteen-man patrol went down hard. Damn, it was Smithson, thought Luke, while firing his M14 at the Vietcong. Another grunt, Martinez, jerked with the impact of bullets; he went down. The white muzzle flashes told Luke they had at least three automatic weapons. He also saw single-shot rifles winking, he heard bullets snapping by.

The enemy rounds were mostly striking near the front of the column. The second fire team was doing a low crawl to the left, behind the rice paddy dikes. The third team crawled to the right; both were trying to flank the enemy as they got out of the kill zone of the ambush. Luke's two machine guns were firing thirty-round bursts at the Vietcong. The tracers were bouncing in crazy red arcs as they hit. The 3.5 rocket team was shooting Willy Peter and high explosive rounds at the enemy's automatic weapons. Boom, BOOM, boom, BOOM.

Luke—a squad leader at only 20 years old—watched his grunts moving; they had been taught well.

The fire team on the right had it easier because their dike was taller and they could scuttle on hands and knees. The other fire team could only move in team rushes: two men shooting, two men moving, two shooting and two moving. The M79 man was thumping his way down the tree line, marking his trail with 40mm explosions: thump, thump.

The whole thing was happening in slow motion, but Luke was moving at normal speed, crouching and firing his rifle while moving toward the radioman. Bent, as they called Benton, was handing the microphone to Luke.

Luke slid down behind the dike; he saw the green tracers zipping overhead and beside him. Bent rolled over and was again shooting at the Vietcong. Luke got on the radio, the sounds of the ambush fading.

"India, India One, ambush at Checkpoint Two."

"India One, India, gotcha, help's on the way. Need eighty-ones?"

"Yeah, south of Checkpoint Two, will correct."

The noise of the battle returned as Luke sat up and continued shooting at the muzzle flashes as he waited for the spotter round.

With a bang and a whooshing sound the 81mm mortar round slammed into the paddy on the other side of the tree line. For a brief instant the exploding round looked like a white Christmas tree. The burning white phosphorus began sizzling into the water.

"Left fifty, fire for effect!" Luke yelled into the microphone.

The mortar's high explosive shells began arriving with their characteristic sizzle-sizzle-whump, whump sound when they exploded. Great gouts of the tree line were being thrown up in the air, branches were flying, shrapnel was making the pit, pit, and pit sounds as it sliced through the underbrush. The smell of gunfire was in the air. After sixteen mortar rounds, they stopped firing.

The Marines kept shooting, although there were fewer muzzle flashes. Luke could hear his men changing rifle magazines; some were throwing grenades at the tree line, the crack sound of them added to the cacophony.

Six VC broke from the right side of the tree line—the seventh was being carried by one of them. The fire team was waiting, and by now a machine gun had joined them. As soon as the enemy came out into the open, the Marines opened fire. The black-clad bodies seemed to be doing a dance as the bullets hit them. They fell in midstride, seven black heaps in the water and mud of the rice paddies.

They had almost made it to the dike that would have protected them from the bullets.

The left fire team got up, fixed bayonets, and began assaulting through the tree line. An occasional burst of rifle fire signaled their finds.

"Fire in the hole," was heard just before a grenade cracked inside the tree line.

"India, India One, I need a medevac, throw some ammo on that bird!"

"India One, Roger—on the way."

The firefight was over and Luke ran to check on his wounded Marines. The first one he came to was Roberto Martinez. No doubt he was dead: one of the rounds had torn a large, jagged hole in his head. The corpsman had put two battle dressings around the wound, but it had continued to bleed. Luke saw more battle dressings on his chest and around his right leg; he noticed the two riflemen from his first fire team were guarding the body. He moved up to Jack Smithson, who had been shot in the neck and through his right arm. The corpsman was tying off the battle dressing around the arm.

Jack was holding a battle dressing tight to his neck—he was still conscious and was trying to smile at Luke. His smile was dreamy looking because he had been given a shot of morphine. It looked like the round had passed through the soft tissue of his neck, didn't hit anything vital.

Luke said, "How you doing, Jack?"

"I got a stiff neck and my arm don't work. Fuck, that's my jacking off hand too."

"Relax, we got a bird on the way, you can learn how to use the other hand at the naval hospital."

"Yeah, round-eyed nurses there."

"I got to check on the rest of the squad. See you later."

"Semper fi," said Jack.

Luke scanned the killing zone and saw the doc working on another Marine on the ground. Luke hadn't noticed him before *and felt guilty as he ran to the Marines clustered around the wounded man.*

It was Nelson and he was dead. The corpsman had quit working on him.

The dead and wounded were lifted out by chopper; the Marines got more ammo. They continued their patrol but were now headed back to the company perimeter. The toll for the Marines was two dead, five wounded. The enemy body count was ten confirmed kills, four wounded and captured.

The patrol was walking through a village when it happened. Luke was looking in a dark hooch when he saw someone running toward him: the Vietcong had a rifle and bayonet and it was pointing at his guts.

Luke's stomach muscles tightened up against the oncoming triangle-shaped bayonet. Just before the sharpened steel touched him …

◇◇◇

Luke came back to the real world. His heart was thumping hard enough to be heard. His sweaty face had a sheen to it.

His flashback happened while he was sitting in the front seat of his squad car. Using the radar gun, Luke was trolling for speeders on the two-lane county road.

The '67 Plymouth had decals on the front doors identifying it as belonging to the Carlton County Sheriff's Department. A 383 was under the hood. Two huge revolving red lights sat on the roof, and a spotlight on the driver's side completed the job.

A Motorola two-way radio hung in the dash, a 12 gauge pump shotgun was clamped upright on the passenger side of the bench seat. The shotgun held four double-aught buck shells and was held in place by an electrical lock. A small silver button under the dash activated the lock; two other switches controlled the car's brake and backup lights. There was a nightstick under the front seat. A six-cell flashlight was wedged in the seat cushions.

Luke was wearing a deputy's uniform: a light brown shirt with a gold star on the left side, a brass nameplate above the shirt pocket. He had long, dark brown pants and Wellington boots. Around his waist was his wide leather gun belt. A .38 caliber M&P Smith & Wesson revolver rode on his right hip. He had a can of Mace on the left side, a nightstick ring, and a pouch on the left front held twelve more rounds of pistol ammo. Another pouch on the back of the belt held his chrome-plated handcuffs. In his briefcase lying on the front seat Luke carried two boxes of .38s, two boxes of shotgun shells. He also had an extra pair of handcuffs in there.

In the trunk of the car Luke had a Savage Bolt-Action .30-06; he had fifty rounds for that heavy caliber rifle.

Luke smiled when he thought back to how he came to be sitting in the squad car.

CHAPTER TWO

It was September of 1967; Luke was twenty-two years old, and had recently been discharged from the Marine Corps after five years' service. He turned down a chance to reenlist for six more years despite the promises that they would teach him Mandarin Chinese at the Defense Language Institute in Monterey, California. He had survived thirteen months of combat and got out as a corporal with an honorable discharge.

He broke up with his longtime girlfriend, Judy, after she said he was drastically changed after the war. They didn't fight; she just said Luke wasn't there anymore. Luke was just numb, no feelings. He was working construction jobs because he liked working outside. Construction paid better than factory jobs anyway.

One evening Luke got a long-distance phone call from his maa. The call was collect, but Luke didn't mind paying for it because he was working and his mother wasn't. Alice Warmwater said, "The sheriff stopped by, looking for you."

"I didn't do anything, maybe drinking too much but nothing illegal."

"No, he wants to hire you; he got some of that LBJ poverty money and wants you as a deputy."

"Uh-huh," replied Luke.

"Think about it and give him a call."

"*Aaniin dash* in the brush?" Luke asked, falling easily into the old habit of Ojibberish, the mix of English and Ojibwe.

"Not much—a couple of funerals, a couple of babies born. We had a good sugar bush, the kids are okay. My dad's dance is next week."

"I can come home for that," Luke promised.

"Think about that deputy thing, it would be good for you to live here."

"I miss the little town of Sawyer since Judy and I broke up."

"Too bad, but she didn't really fit in. She laughed too much or not enough or at the wrong time."

"It wasn't her fault she was raised white. She said I was too different after the war, said I wasn't the Luke she knew."

"You will find a new girlfriend," she said. "More and more guys from the Rez are going to Vietnam; your brother Wabegan wants to go."

"No more for me, thanks. Tell Wabegan *gego*—don't," Luke said, while spitting out a short laugh.

"Call the sheriff, and oh, yeah—watch that drinking shit."

"Yeah, I'm tired of Portsmouth, Ohio, anyway."

"Come home, then," she said.

"Okay, Maa, see you next time."

"Or the time after next," she replied.

The following week Luke drove home to Sawyer. He greeted his maa and dad.

"You can have the couch all to yourself while you're here," Maa said.

Luke laughed as he saw his maa cooking food to help out for her dad's dance. This was a big event in the little village of Sawyer. They had only two of these ceremonies a year.

His grandfather had rented a large tent for the doings. The bright colors told Luke this tent had once been part of a carnival somewhere. Since he was young, strong, and had experience in erecting shelters and tents in Vietnam, Luke helped raise it.

Indians were arriving from all nearby Reservations. There was a lot of laughter as the people began visiting, and a lot of what was said was in Ojibwe. Luke understood quite a bit but was hesitant about speaking it. He vividly remembered being punished for using Ojibwe words when he was in Pipestone, the federal boarding school. When someone spoke to him in Ojibwe he answered in English.

Luke wanted to feel the drum beating against his chest again. As he settled into his chair to watch the proceedings, he saw two young women come in. Luke knew they weren't from this Rez, so he went up and introduced himself.

"*Boozhoo*, I'm Luke Warmwater, welcome to Sawyer." He shook hands with both of them. Right away he preferred looking and talking to the bolder one of the two, who said, "I'm Carrie East from Grand Portage. I go to University of Wisconsin–Superior. We heard about this dance." Pointing the woman next to her, Carrie said, "She is my friend from school—this is Meganikwe Brown from the Bad River Reservation in Wisconsin."

"Carrie East, isn't your last name Meeback?" Luke asked.

She laughed and said, "Nope, it's East," pointing with her lips in an easterly direction. Instantly Luke wanted to kiss those lips.

Luke said, "Let's talk some more when it's time to eat. I'll save you a couple of seats."

"*Mii gwech*," said Carrie. She looked down and saw he wasn't wearing a wedding ring. Who is this guy? she thought.

The singers began on the drum. Different ones got up and danced, but most just stayed in the circle of chairs and benches around the drum. The strong drumbeat reached everyone; old ladies would frequently stand up and dance in place, then sit back down. Luke knew these were members of the drum.

Every time he looked at Carrie across the tent, she was looking at him and smiling. And each time she looked at him she saw him looking at her. His big grin told her all she needed to know.

When it was time for the evening meal Luke met the two women at the table. The food was in the middle; the meal had been prepared by the women in the community. Luke and his two new friends ate wild rice, fry bread, deer, moose, and rabbit. They continued visiting, and Luke asked Carrie if he could see her again. She smiled yes.

After the dance Luke went home. He saw his maa washing dishes in the kitchen. He sat at the table and said, "I think I met someone."

"I know, I saw you two throwing eyes at each other all night."

"Her name is Carrie East. She's from Grand Portage."

"Who was her friend?"

"Meganikwe Brown from Bad River. I'm going to meet Carrie next week."

"Okay, Mr. Romance, don't forget to call the sheriff about becoming a deputy."

Luke and Carrie went out to eat and made plans to meet again and again. Luke told her of his plans to become a deputy. He told her he had to call Sheriff Johnson the next day.

Luke remembered the call and that meeting with the sheriff. They met in the sheriff's office in Carlton.

Ralph Johnson was the elected sheriff. He had been the chief deputy when Luke left for boot camp some years back. Ralph was in his late thirties, and Luke knew him from when he was growing up on the Rez.

They drank coffee together as they talked about the sheriff's job offer.

"I'd like you to join the sheriff's department, and become a sworn deputy of mine," said Ralph. "Interested?"

"Could be. I was a military policeman for a year and a half before I went to Vietnam," replied Luke. "I liked that work; tell me about this job."

"The duties are to enforce the state law in this county—we're sometimes called to assist nearby counties because we have mutual aid agreements. There are about twenty-eight thousand people in the county.

"We have six other deputies—four on the road, one deputy who handles civil affairs like subpoenas, and one chief deputy. Then, we have three jailers who also dispatch the squad cars. The city of Cloquet has ten sworn police officers, and there are two Minnesota state highway patrolmen who mostly work in this county. Questions about any of this?"

"No, but I always thought there were more deputies than that," said Luke.

"Well, we have a group of volunteers called the Rescue Squad, about twenty of them, and they help out with traffic control, searches, and sometimes they ride with the deputies on patrol."

"I see, and where would I fit in?"

"We'd like you to be a road deputy, but you'd start off working with the jailers—you'd learn how the jail operates, what logs are kept, how to dispatch the squad cars. Calls come in on the phone or radio, you log all of your activities. I'd like you to start once we get your uniforms and equipment. We provide your gun belt and everything you need, including hand-cuffs, a nightstick, a thirty-eight caliber pistol, ammunition and keys—the keys will fit the back door of the jail—squad-car keys, handcuff keys, and a key for the cabinet that holds all of the keys you'll need.

"We have a contract with a clothing store in Duluth where you'll get measured for your uniforms. Go down there tomorrow morning and they'll have your uniforms ready the following day. What do you say?"

"I think yes, Sheriff Johnson."

"Excellent. I'm glad to have you as a deputy, Luke. You'll meet the other employees of the sheriff's department in the next couple of days."

"This sounds interesting. Maybe exciting," said Luke.

"It's always interesting but not very exciting—although once in a while we have our moments," the sheriff replied.

"Remember, you will always be in the public eye, my representative. And there is one other thing we have to talk about. In a word: racism. There are a lot of people in this county who don't like Indians. Do you think you can handle that?"

"I can handle just about anything as long as they're not shooting at me," said Luke.

"So, even if they were members of the sheriff's department?"

"I met a lot of different kinds of guys in the Marine Corps, all different races, some I would call racists. But after being together for a while that stuff sort of fell away. Guys who didn't know me called me Chief, but the ones I trained and fought with knew me by my name," answered Luke.

"Perhaps we can change some attitudes around here, since I know you're not going to change being Indian. We need an attitude adjustment in the sheriff's department. You'll be the first Indian that ever worked here, you know."

"No, I didn't know that," said Luke. "Does that make me a pioneer?"

"I don't know about pioneer, but you'll be a first for Carlton County."

"Then I believe I am honored."

"Your mother said you were in combat in Vietnam. How was it?"

"I guess I would call it boring and exciting. Mostly it was boring, but when it was exciting it was really exciting. There was a half-second in between the two—boring and exciting," explained Luke.

"Did you have to kill anyone?"

"Yeah, I got a personal body count, but I don't talk about it much."

"I can understand," said the sheriff. "We had a shoot-out here a couple of years ago down in Moose Lake."

"What happened?"

"I was serving divorce papers on a man, working with the Moose Lake constable. We came into the driveway and the man inside started shooting at us with a deer rifle. The first round came through the windshield, blinding the constable. I was trying to get out of the squad car, had my door open but forgot to take my seat belt off. The second round came through the door, took out a chunk of my left forearm."

With that, the sheriff rolled up his sleeve and Luke saw the chunk of muscle missing from his arm. It looked like a healed gunshot wound. Luke looked closer because he had never seen healed ones, only bloody ones.

Luke rolled up his pants leg where he had several shrapnel scars. He told the sheriff about his wounds.

"We were in a firefight, I was running when I heard a loud explosion. I didn't feel anything so I kept running. After everything was over, we were sitting around talking about what happened when I noticed blood on my trouser leg. I saw several holes and saw some chunks of shrapnel sticking out of my leg. The corpsman came over and pulled the big chunks out of my leg with a hemostat—that kind of stung. He used that green Phisohex soap and cleaned me up. He put a battle dressing on and said he would write me up for a Purple Heart. I told him I didn't want one because we called those Idiot Awards. It didn't matter anyway, because the corpsman was killed that night by a mortar round."

"Idiot Awards?" asked the sheriff.

"Yeah, it meant you were standing in the wrong place at the wrong time and got hit."

"Any more holes?"

"Yeah, got a couple in my back too."

"Yup, sounds like you were in a war. Hopefully you won't add any more holes to your body."

"I think it would be nice if you didn't either," said Luke.

"Let me tell you about what you'll be doing, then."

"Okay, I'm ready."

"Just check in with Si—Si Maki—he'll show you the ropes. You don't have to do anything, just watch what Si does as a jailer. I already told him I thought you'd be starting soon."

"Okay, I can do that."

"We call it OJT: on-the-job training. We will send you to police school in Duluth later, but this will get you started. Oh, yeah, by the way—we work twelve-hour shifts."

"I can do that," said Luke. Uh-oh, he thought, now what has Bope and Alice's oldest son got himself into? He had had the same thought when he went back to his decision to join the Marine Corps, when he had hooked up with his girlfriend Judy, and now when he decided to join the Carlton County Sheriff's Department.

When Luke picked up his uniforms he tried one on as soon as he got home. He wondered when he would get his badge to hang on the reinforced portion of the shirt; his brass nameplate was on order and he would begin wearing that as soon as it arrived. Luke put on his gun belt, the weight of it around his hips reminding him of the cartridge belt he used to wear in Vietnam. This one was lighter, though, because he didn't have heavy rifle bullets or two quarts of water hanging from it. He tried a quick draw with his pistol, then loaded it with six rounds.

He put the nightstick on his left side and tried drawing out his handcuffs from the pouch on the right rear of the gun belt. The last step was to put on his hat with the shiny brass star in front. Luke looked into his mirror, studied his image while thinking about his new career. He felt ready.

CHAPTER THREE

Luke had found a small house to rent that was a block from the jail. On his first day, he walked through the alley to work, left his personal vehicle at home. The new deputy rang the bell at the jail office.

Si Maki threw his hands up in mock surrender when he saw him, then laughed and invited him in. Luke was scheduled to work from 1500, or 3:00 P.M., until 0300, or 3:00 A.M. Luke was glad to see the sheriff's department used the military designation for telling time.

Si showed him where the coffeepot was located—he also showed him where they kept the cans of coffee and the extra cups in the jail kitchen. They sat at the table and had a cup of coffee. The sheriff apparently heard Luke come in, so he came to the kitchen.

Ralph shook hands with his new deputy and said, "Welcome aboard. Did you get all of your uniforms and equipment?" Luke stood up and showed the sheriff how he looked.

"You won't need the gun belt on while you're working with Si. Put it in your locker over there. C'mon into the other office and meet my secretary, Alvina Pearl Larson. She knows where everything is. She's the real boss of this place."

Luke walked into her office and the sheriff introduced him to Alvina. Luke saw a distinguished-looking woman, about forty-five years old. She got up from behind her desk and came around to shake hands with Luke. She had a big smile on her face as she grabbed his hand in a powerful grip. Her blue eyes seemed to sparkle as they shook hands. "Call me Pearl because I hate the name Alvina," she said.

The sheriff continued, "If you need anything, or have a question about something, just ask Pearl."

Pearl nodded her head in agreement and pointed out the bank of file cabinets. She explained that they held all of the sheriff's office records going back twenty years or so. "The key to the file cabinet is in my main desk drawer; use it if you want to read a recent history of our department." She also pointed out a stack of law enforcement magazines and catalogs, among which Luke noticed the monthly magazine sent by the FBI.

Luke walked with the sheriff back to the jail office. He stood tall while Sheriff Johnson pinned the badge on his shirt. He could hardly wait to show his maa and dad. He thought they would be proud of him.

The sheriff handed him a set of keys on a string. "Here are the keys you'll need. That ignition key fits all of the squad cars, this is the key to the back door of the jail, and this is the key for the cabinet over there," he explained, pointing over his shoulder at the cabinet on the jail's kitchen wall. "Inside, you'll find the cellblock keys for the two downstairs; the two other big brass ones are for the juvenile cell and the women's cells upstairs. There's also a key for the basement, where we keep our evidence locker."

Luke was absorbing the information when the sheriff continued, "I'll take you out to the gravel pit on Monday—it's the one we use for a rifle range. You can test-fire your pistol, fire one of the shotguns and the tear-gas launcher."

Luke looked forward to the smell of gun smoke, He wondered how frequently he would smell that particular smell again. He thought back to when he last smelled gun smoke, then quickly banished it from his mind. No sense thinking about that war now, he thought.

Oh, but the war is there, always lurking just beneath the surface, the memories etched deep.

As Luke and Si settled into the jail routine, Si explained, "We got nine prisoners downstairs in the cellblocks. Upstairs there are two women, no juveniles."

Si showed Luke the two-way radio system and the Teletype that could connect with other sheriff's departments in the state. The machine was also connected to the state highway patrol and to another office that kept track of motor vehicle registrations and people who had outstanding warrants.

Si and Luke delivered the evening meals to the prisoners. In looking over the jail book, Luke saw that one of his uncles and two cousins were currently confined there.

Calls for assistance came into the jail office, and Si would dispatch either the deputy that patrolled the southern half of the county or the one working the more heavily populated northern half of the county. If it looked serious, Si would send both squads to the scene, and if was really serious, he would call the sheriff at home and the other deputies too.

Luke thought it would take him a long time to learn all that went on in the operation of the jail. Si told him it would get a lot busier during the weekends.

For now, they sat at the desks and traded life stories. Luke learned Si had been working as a jailer for the past eighteen years. He was fifty-five years old and had been a road deputy until he thought he was too old to be wrestling drunks out there.

Luke told Si he had joined the Marine Corps right out of high school and had been out for just over a year. He didn't say anything about Vietnam. He also told him he was from Sawyer, the little village ten miles west of the jail. It turned out Si knew quite a few people from Sawyer. Si would say a name and Luke would tell him how he was related to that person.

Then Si showed him the various records that were kept. He also explained the procedure for when a prisoner was brought in, showed him how to take three sets of fingerprints. One set was kept in the sheriff's office, one set was sent to the Bureau of

Criminal Apprehension in St. Paul, and one was mailed to the FBI in Washington, D.C. Si also showed Luke how to take mug shot pictures.

The hours ticked by and Si explained how they shut off the lights in the cellblocks at 2200. Both settled into the evening and night routine at the Carlton County Jail. Every fifteen minutes or so, Si checked the cellblocks for anything unusual.

At 2216, a radio alerted them that Deputy 103 was coming in with a prisoner. In the ten-code talk it came across as 103 is 10-8 with a 10-15. Luke found a ten-code card and began memorizing the list.

"One-oh-three is Roy Brant; he was in the southern half of the county tonight," Si informed Luke.

"Carlton County, one-oh-three, I'm outside the front door."

With that Luke got up to unlock the door with his big brass key. He opened the door and watched the deputy bringing in his prisoner. They were wandering back and forth coming up the sidewalk. Luke guessed drunk driver. He didn't know the prisoner.

Deputy Roy Brant came into the jail, still holding his prisoner's arm. "I think we can hold off on the prints and photos until tomorrow morning, let the day shift do it."

Luke looked at Roy and saw a rather short-looking man, about five feet six, weighing about two hundred pounds—a sardonic looking little man. He appeared to be about thirty and walked hard, his feet making a loud noise on the floor. He held his head as if expecting a slap at any time.

Si nodded, filled out the arrest record, and searched the prisoner before taking the cuffs off and leading him to the cellblock. He gave him a thin brown blanket. Using his brass key, Si opened the door, stepped back as the prisoner entered the cellblock.

Deputy Brant came back into the office after getting a cup of coffee. He looked at Luke and said, "Who are you? I'm Roy Brant."

"I'm Luke Warmwater, just started working here today."

"I didn't know they let you people in the sheriff's department," Brant sneered.

"You people?" asked Luke. He could feel his muscles tensing.

"Yeah, you guys—those of the Indian persuasion."

"Well, a new day is dawning," Luke told him tersely.

Brant just shook his head, smirking to himself. He picked up his handcuffs and headed out the door.

Si came walking over to where they were standing and said, "Okay Luke, see how that was done? Ordinarily we take prints and a couple of pictures, then we search them before taking the cuffs off. They're usually pretty tame once we start walking them to the cellblock door, but once in awhile we get someone who wants to wrestle when they get in here. Now we enter the information in this log," Si said, showing Luke the green cloth-bound book. He entered the time, date, prisoner's name, charge, and the arresting deputy's name and badge number. "It's usually pretty quiet during the week, but during the weekend we'll do this eight to ten times a shift."

"Okay, so then we just wait for the next phone call or radio message?"

"Yup. Usually pretty quiet. C'mon, I'll show you how to work the Teletype."

Si demonstrated how to send a message to St. Paul, asking for a 10-28, 29. From his earlier studying, Luke knew that meant a registration or stolen check based on a license plate. He knew he would quickly learn the ten-code by using it.

"Did Roy really say 'you people'?"

"Yeah, I thought he was trying to put me in my place," answered Luke.

"Get used to it—you'll be hearing that kind of thing a lot here. How did you handle it before?"

"Well, it usually ended up in a fistfight. In Vietnam I would have just stuck my Ka-Bar knife in his neck, then twisted and cut on the way out as I was trained," joked Luke, with a slight laugh.

Si looked at him a long time, wondering how close to serious he was. "Yeah, get used to it," he advised. Then he stretched out in an old recliner chair, tucked his head into a pillow. "Wake me if you get a call."

Luke shuddered at the idea of sleeping on watch. He knew he would be awake until the shift ended at 0300.

At 2313, Luke heard the radio: "One-zero-six, county, ten-eight with a ten-fifteen."

From listening to Si earlier, Luke knew how to use the radio. He said, "County, one-zero-six, ETA?"

"I'm about five minutes out."

"Ten-four." Luke knew 106 was the deputy on the north side of the county. He looked at Si, who was smiling with approval as he got up, scratched himself, and went for another cup of coffee. Luke logged in the radio call. He was learning.

Si came back in the office and said, "One-oh-six is Jim Cuffy. He worked his way up as a road deputy by serving in the Rescue Squad. I bet he has our second drunk driver of the shift."

Sure enough, Si was right. Deputy Cuffy escorted in their second drunk prisoner of the night. Luke didn't recognize him. He looked at the deputy, saw a tall—six feet two at least—Swedish-looking man with blond hair, blue eyes. He looked athletic. He moved lightly and had a ready smile.

Si showed Luke how to take the fingerprints, photograph and search the prisoner, and then uncuff his hands.

Cuffy took the man's driver's license out of his shirt pocket and read, "This is Thomas Hautoloma, date of birth February twenty-sixth, nineteen fifty, lives on Birch Street in Cloquet. He had a case of beer on the seat beside him. He said he was just driving around because he was mad at his girlfriend and his mother. I found him headed north on Reservation Road. Tom told me he wasn't drunk, but I was pretty sure he needed a place to sleep tonight."

Si issued the prisoner a blanket and opened the cell. Thomas walked in singing something by the Kingston Trio called "Tijuana Jail."

The three men sat at the kitchen table, coffee poured and blowed.

"The sheriff told me you'd be starting today. He also said you were a Marine," said Cuffy.

"Still am a Marine," said Luke.

"Me too. Did a four-year tour as a wing wiper.

"I was zero-three-eleven, a grunt."

"I spent my time in Cherry Point, El Toro, and Miramar Naval Air Station."

"I got to travel quite a bit with my uncle—my Uncle Sam," said Luke. "I did my last tour with India Company, Third Battalion, Ninth Marines."

"Ninth Marines, eh? So that means you were in Vietnam."

"Yeah, I got out last September, we were at An Hoa."

"Good, we have something in common—we're both Marines."

"Yup, we're wearing a different kind of uniform now, different weapons, but still standing watch."

"I hadn't thought of it that way," said Jim. "Okay, I got to go save the world from the criminal element—let's talk again." With that, Jim put on his hat and was unsnapping his keys from his gun belt. He walked toward the back door, where he stopped, did an about-face, and gave Luke a sharp-looking Marine Corps hand salute. Luke stood up, returned the salute.

It got quiet in the jail and Si went back to sleep in his recliner. Luke made a check of the cellblocks and all was silent. He went into the offices next door and picked up the magazines he had seen earlier in Pearl's office. The phone and the radio were quiet.

He avidly read the law enforcement magazines until it was time to make another walking tour of the cellblocks—it reminded him of checking his troops on the perimeter in An Hoa, South Vietnam.

Luke woke up Si, as the next shift jailer came in the back door. Si sat up, rubbed his face, stretched a good fifteen seconds. He introduced the two.

"Val, this is Luke Warmwater, a new hire, he'll be working with us in the jail before he goes out on the road."

Val, a skinny guy, maybe 140 pounds tops, smiled and shook hands with Luke. He was about five feet nine, the same height as Luke. He said, "Warmwater, eh? Are you related to ... to ...?"

"Yeah, I'm related to all of them," answered Luke before Val could think of a front name.

"Welcome to Carlton County, although I've heard some people call it Cartoon County," smiled Val, beaming at his own little joke.

Si gave Val a status report: number of prisoners, where they were sleeping, an overview of the night's activities.

Val checked the key cabinet and asked Luke, "Are you going to put your brass keys away before you leave?"

"Oh, yeah—thanks for reminding me."

"Oops, I forgot to tell you that part," Si said. "Luke, don't take the jail keys home."

"You two jailers will train me just fine," said Luke. "I'll see you tomorrow night then," he added.

He walked home through the quiet alley. Once home, he took off his gun belt and hat, checked his perimeter—the doors and windows were all locked—put his .38 on the nightstand, laid his nightstick on the floor within easy reach, and crawled into bed.

There were wounded Marines; his squad was sent to protect the wounded as two corpsmen worked on them. To get there they had to run through the mud and water of the rice paddy, with tracers zipping by sporadically. Luke started across. His right boot stuck in the muck; he pulled it up and stepped with his left foot. That one got stuck in the mud. He kept trying to run.

He was running in a crouched position because of the shells going by. It was hard to run like that. Luke turned and looked at his squad running behind him; they didn't use the rice paddy dikes. Those were usually mined and they were too high, up where the bullets were flying by. The VC kept shooting at them. The Marines continued running through the mud.

Luke and his squad reached the wounded Marines and set up a perimeter around them. The VC shooting seemed to slow down. Luke went to help the corpsmen with the wounded. The first one he came to had a gunshot wound through his right upper arm. A corpsman threw Luke a battle dressing. Luke ripped the plastic bag apart to get to the dressing inside; he wrapped it tightly around the Marine's arm. The bleeding slowed down so Luke moved to the next man lying there.

This one had been hit with something that split the skin on his lower belly. A loop of intestine had popped out—about four inches of coiled gut. The Marine was moaning and almost unconscious. Luke kept the man's hands from touching the protrusion. He put on a battle dressing and poured water from his canteen on the wound. Smelling the inside of the man was something Luke had never smelled before. He knew he would never forget that smell.

The shooting had died down, so Luke used the radio to call for a medevac. There were four wounded; one looked dead. In the words of their grizzled old gunnery sergeant, Luke thought: four Popsicles, one of them melted. He remembered the smells.

CHAPTER FOUR

Luke woke up with that body smell stuck in his nostrils. He blew his nose a couple of times and went back to sleep. He slept the way he usually did: out for two hours, up for a few minutes, slept for two hours and woke up for a couple of minutes as if he were still back in Vietnam. He only woke up with two nightmares that night. He didn't know if he had nightmares that didn't wake him.

In the morning Luke showered and put on his uniform again, buckled his gun belt, and looked at himself in the mirror. He went outside and locked his door.

When he got into his car he decided to visit his maa and dad in Sawyer. While making the drive west on Highway 210, Luke thought about what their faces would look like when he walked in wearing a deputy's uniform.

When he got home he saw a couple of brothers and a nephew playing in a dirt pile on the side of the house. It was Buckshot, Wabegan, and Meat. They looked at the strange car driving up and saw Luke get out of his car. He was watching them when his brother Buckshot said, "Cops," and took off running into the brush. The other two ran off in different directions. From the woods Luke could hear one of them yelling, "Dirty copper, dirty copper!"

Luke smiled and went into the house. His maa was sitting at the kitchen table drinking coffee and having a smoke. His dad was there, and when he saw his son in a uniform, he stood up, put his hands up, and leaned into the wall as if he was ready to be searched. He laughed out loud and sat back down at the table.

"You look like a real deputy," Maa said while looking at his uniform and gun belt. "*Makademashkiikiiwaaboo na?*" she asked, while pouring a cup of coffee and opening a tin that held a freshly baked cake. She put a piece of cake on a plate, reached behind, and gave him a fork.

"Yeah, I'll have some coffee, still drink it just black."

"I am proud of you, son," said his dad. "I'd like to admire you and your uniform but I got to go to the woods, those trees aren't cutting themselves, and these kids got to eat every day."

"*Mii gwech*," Luke told his dad.

On the way out the door his dad stopped and said, "Maybe you can stop the deputies from beating up these Indians. Happens every time someone gets arrested."

"I'll stop it if it happens in front of me. I am Anishinaabe before I am a deputy," Luke assured his dad.

Outside Luke could hear his dad yelling at his brothers still hiding in the brush, "Go inside and see your brother. Don't piss him off, or he'll take you to jail."

The boys came in awkwardly and quietly, lining up on the wall farthest from Luke. Finally Wabegan got brave and asked, "Is that a real gun?"

"Yup, do some work for your maa and I'll let you shoot it. What you got for these young boys to do?" Luke asked his maa.

She stretched and using just her lips, pointed at the backyard and said, "Someone has to drag that brush out in the woods," she said. "We're trying to make the yard bigger so the mosquitoes won't be so bad."

The boys ran outside and began dragging the brush deep into the woods. His maa said, "How's that Carrie girl? And when do we meet her?"

"She's okay, I'll bring her around one of these days."

"Yeah, okay, does she cook?"

"I think so, she was telling me how much she missed it because she was living in the dorm," he said. His maa smiled.

Luke got up, went outside, and got a box of .38 caliber rounds from his car.

Alice Warmwater raised the window and said, "*Weweni*—be careful."

Luke found an old coffee can and set it up on a stump. He took out the pistol and showed the boys where the trigger was, the front and back sights. He cautioned the boys, "Death comes out of here," pointing at the end of the barrel. "Understand?"

The three boys nodded in agreement. Luke smiled at them. "Hold the sights on the target and just slowly squeeze the trigger. Don't jerk it back—slowly squeeze the trigger."

Luke fired off three rounds, hit the coffee can once, then twice. The boys clapped their hands over their ears as the pistol went off.

Buckshot gingerly held the pistol; Luke had his hands on top of the young boy's hands. He let go and said, "Keep the sights on the can, slowly squeeze the trigger."

For every round fired by the young boys, Luke fired two. They didn't know it but he was getting used to shooting that .38. He used up a box of shells before he ended the unplanned gun safety lesson.

As the boys ran off he heard Buckshot say, "I almost hit the coffee can that one time."

"Did not, you jerked the trigger."

Luke went back inside to visit with his maa. There was a new piece of cake waiting on his saucer. He refilled his coffee cup and sat at the kitchen table.

Alice looked at her oldest son and said, "How is it working at the jail?"

"There sure is a lot to learn there."

"You learn fast," she said, "Look how you got promoted in the Marine Corps."

"I learned one guy doesn't like me—doesn't even know me and he doesn't like me."

"Let me guess, is he the one named Brant?

"Yeah, he asked me what one of 'you people' was doing in his sheriff's department."

"Who else did you meet?"

"I work with the jailer, Si Maki—he seems okay. Oh, yeah, I met Jim Cuffy—he was a wing-wiping Marine. Jim was working the north half of the county. The next shift jailer, Val, seemed nice."

"Some of those deputies act like humans and others are pretty strict. I guess your dad has wrestled with all of them over the years."

Luke ate his cake and finished his coffee. He got up and headed for the door. Maa's eyes said she was proud of him as he walked outside to get in his car.

Just as Luke was about to open the car door he heard his mother say, "*Bekaa.*"

He waited as his mother came out of the house and walked up to stand next to him. When their eyes met she said, "I want to smudge you."

With that she lit one end of the braided sweetgrass. Luke stood up, relaxed his hands at his side. She was using an eagle feather to fan the smoke toward her son's body. When she came in front of him, he grabbed at the smoke, washed his face with it, also his hair. The ceremony was brief but powerful.

"You know, if a deputy was to take a ride down toward the *manoomin* landing at Perch Lake, he might find something interesting along the way."

Luke laughed and he knew that was all his maa was going to say on that subject.

He drove west on Moorhead Road, crested a small hill, and saw something on the side of the road. As he got closer he could see it was a car. There was no one around and Luke looked it over. It was a white Lincoln Continental, a 1965—Luke got the year number from the taillights. The year was part of the code on the bottom of the lens. It was a four-door and the license plates were missing.

The car was sitting on the hubs, tires and wheels were missing, and under the hood he could see the battery and carburetor were gone—also the radiator. Inside the car there was broken car-window glass on the seats and the radio was missing. Two of the windows were broken.

He wrote down the VIN and got into his car. He drove to the Sawyer store, which had a pay phone, and called the sheriff's office. He tried to mimic talking on the phone as if it were a radio.

"Carlton County Sheriff's Office," the dispatcher answered.

"One-zero-four, county, I got a possible stolen car on west Moorhead Road in Sawyer. The VIN is Whiskey seventy-nine, Romeo thirty-seven, fifty-two Juliet, sixty-five, thirty-nine."

Luke waited.

"County, one-oh-four, that's a hit. It was listed as stolen from Saint Paul last week."

"One-zero-four, county, ten-four, I'll wait here for the tow truck."

While waiting Luke was thinking about the whole thing. He knew his maa knew who was driving the car before it was stripped, who had the battery and tires, who had the radiator and carburetor. He knew she knew all about it but also knew she wouldn't tell him that part.

Once back at the jail, Luke noted that the jailer had logged in the incident as a recovered stolen vehicle. While walking through, the sheriff complimented him for the recovery, even though he was off-duty.

Luke went to his house in Carlton and slept for a couple of hours. He wasn't sure if he had a nightmare or not. He was looking forward to going to work that afternoon. He thought that seemed strange—looking forward to going to jail.

CHAPTER FIVE

Two months passed by. The flashbacks and nightmares from Vietnam continued. Carrie and Luke saw each other more frequently. They laughed together many times.

"Is it okay if I call you my girlfriend?"

"Only if I can call you my man," she replied.

"I'll call you my woman then."

As Luke was getting ready to get in his car, the approaching headlights told him a logging truck was bearing down on him. He closed his door and stood back out of the way.

"That was a close one," he said, getting in the car.

"I'm afraid of those things—too big, too scary."

Luke was familiar with all of the happenings at the jail. He had locked up a couple of his cousins and one uncle. He noticed there always seemed to be a lot of Indians in jail. He had read all the crime reports held by the sheriff's department going back twenty-one years.

At home he had a couple of nightmares. One was very detailed and he remembered waking up confused; another was vague but he woke up being very afraid of something. No flashbacks, however—no major ones, anyway.

One evening Luke was working with Si when a telephone call alerted them to a problem in Sawyer.

"Shots fired at Yakker's Tavern," said Si, excitement making his voice louder.

Sheriff Johnson was in his office and heard Si's report. It was 2315. He came into the jail office, caught Luke's eyes, and said, "Grab your gun belt and hat, you'll be riding with me."

Luke had been waiting for an event like this—he wanted to be out on the road. "Ten-four," he told the sheriff.

The sheriff was driving his unmarked squad car. Luke got into the passenger seat and buckled up.

"We'll take a quick look at the scene, the bar. But I think everyone's gone by now. We'll get Bob and Rose's version of what happened later," the sheriff said.

"Do we know who's involved?

"Bob told me on the phone. Bill Wildman and the Carney boys from Cloquet were fighting. Someone's headed to the hospital because one of them got cut punching out Bill's window. Bill shot the chimney and fired in the air a couple of times before the Carney boys decided to leave."

They quickly arrived in Sawyer and began looking for Bill's car. They checked his house first—no sign of anyone moving around. They went to his usual places because both the sheriff and Luke knew them.

"I think he's still driving that green fifty-seven Chevy," said the sheriff. They continued looking in the quiet village. "I remember now—he has a girlfriend from Cromwell, maybe we should take a look there," he continued.

They headed west on Highway 210, Cromwell was ten miles west of Sawyer.

The sheriff and his deputy could see a car's headlights approaching from the west. The sheriff slowed down to sixty miles an hour.

"Eight Mary, forty-three fifty. Nope, that isn't Bill's car." Luke was amazed that the sheriff could read the oncoming car's front license plate at that speed on the dark highway.

"How'd you do that, Sheriff?" asked Luke.

"Years of experience and quick eyes," he replied.

After a mile or so they could see another car approaching, a solitary headlight lit up the highway.

"I don't know if Bill's car has a headlight out, we'll see in a minute or two. Can you use that shotgun?"

"Yeah, I carried one like this a year ago in the 'Nam."

"Might have to take out a tire if he runs," advised the sheriff.

"Eight Mary, zero forty-two four," said the sheriff as they met the car. "That's Bill."

Luke swiveled in his seat and assured the sheriff, "I'm watching him."

The sheriff reached down and switched off the brake and backup lights on his squad car. He jammed on the brakes hard and pulled over to the side of the road. He cut the wheels sharply and backed up fast. When the front wheels were far enough back he hit the brakes and slid around facing toward Bill's car. He punched down on the gas pedal and the engine roared.

"Highway patrol turn," he explained. He continued holding the gas pedal down and they began to gain on the Chevy. It didn't take very long to catch up.

Sheriff Johnson took a fireball off the floor, put it on the dashboard, and a revolving red light swept the back of the fleeing car.

"He isn't stopping," said the sheriff.

"Ten-four," said Luke.

The squad car stayed right behind the Chevy. When the sheriff pulled into the left lane to pass, the driver moved in front of him. Luke glanced at the speedometer: they were doing better than seventy miles an hour.

After trying to get alongside of the car, the sheriff asked Luke, "Ready with that shotgun?"

"Yes."

Luke quickly realized he'd have a better shot from inside the car if he shot left-handed. He was ready.

The sheriff finally got close to being alongside the car. He told his deputy, "Take out the rear tire."

"Ten-four."

The sheriff was speeding up; Billy was jamming on his brakes. Luke saw the rear fender, rear tire, and Billy all in the same second. "Boom," said Luke's shotgun. He pulled the slide back and forth, ejecting the spent round and loading a fresh one in the chamber.

The Chevy limped over to the side of the road. The sheriff stopped his car on the left-rear side of the Chevy. Luke got out and stuck the shotgun barrel in Bill's ear. "Don't move, put your hands where I can see them."

Bill complied and draped his hands over the steering wheel. There was a strong smell of alcohol coming from the inside of the car.

"Where's the rifle?" demanded Luke.

"Under the front seat," answered Bill.

Luke ripped open the front door, reached down, and pulled out the rifle by the butt. He let it fall to the ground and put one foot on it. He told Bill, "Get out of the car and put your hands on the roof." Bill complied again. Luke kept his shotgun pointed at him.

The sheriff came up, did a quick body search, and put handcuffs on Bill. He explained, "If they're dangerous enough to be cuffed, they're dangerous enough to be cuffed with their hands behind them."

Luke picked up the rifle and unloaded it, putting the shells in his jacket pocket. When he was done, he put the rifle in the squad car. He looked in the backseat of the Chevy and saw two human shapes. They appeared to be asleep, but Luke thought they were faking. It's tough to sleep through a high-speed chase and a shotgun blast.

Luke grabbed an ankle and rolled it back and forth, "Get up and get out of the car, this side, I want to see your hands." As the first one came out of the car Luke continued, "Put your hands on the fender."

The second one climbed out, and Luke gave the same order. He pointed his shotgun at the two people, one was a woman. The sheriff had put Billy in the backseat, left the dome light on. Bill was hunched over, slowly shaking his head no.

The sheriff came up to search the two people leaning on the fender. He started with the man. The man turned and Luke was surprised to see he was pointing his shotgun at his own uncle— the one they called Besaa, his maa's oldest brother. He lowered his shotgun.

The sheriff searched the woman when Luke's uncle spoke. "Holy Christ, Sheriff, what's happening? Her and me were just trying to pass out in the back of Billy's car."

"We'll talk about it when we get back to the jail," the sheriff replied.

"Who you got riding with you tonight?" Besaa turned around to see Luke with his shotgun now pointed up in the air. "*Niningwanis*, when did you start riding in a squad car? I heard you were a jailer," Besaa said to his nephew.

"Tonight's my first time," answered Luke.

"You got a smoke?" Besaa took his hands off the fender and came strolling over to stand next to his nephew on that dark Minnesota highway. Luke took out his cigarette pack with his left hand and shook out a cigarette for his uncle.

"Got one for her too?" asked his uncle as Esther turned and came over to join the group. Luke didn't know her very well but knew she was from the Cloquet side of the Rez. He shook out a smoke for her.

The sheriff leaned into the backseat of the squad and asked Billy, "You got a spare tire, Bill?"

"Yeah, got one in the trunk."

Then he told Luke, "Change that tire so we don't have to call for a tow truck. Drive Billy's car to the jail and we can start writing the reports."

"Ten-four," said Luke.

He started to put his shotgun in the sheriff's car and the sheriff cautioned him, "Better jack another shell in the chamber, I didn't hear you reload."

Luke slid the slide back and forth. A fresh shell ejected and fell on the front seat; he had done it automatically. He loaded the fresh round back in the shotgun.

The sheriff smiled. "I'll drop those two off in Sawyer on my way to jail with Billy. They didn't do any shooting, only Billy."

"Ten-four," said Luke.

The sheriff was talking on the radio as they left. Luke was standing on the side of the dark highway. Glad I didn't keep shooting after the first round, he thought. That was how he solved his problems the year before in the 'Nam: a final round in the head to make sure.

Luke changed the tire with the aid of the stars and a flashlight and drove Bill's car to the county jail. He opened the passenger-side window along with the driver's window. He was using the wind to blow the alcohol smell from the car.

Once there, he parked Billy's car in the sheriff's parking lot and used his key to go in the back door of the jail. He found the sheriff sitting at the table writing his report.

"I don't know if I should mention this or not, but I'm not an actual sworn deputy yet," said Luke.

"I was swearing you in as you were aiming at that car, didn't you hear me?"

"No, your siren was blaring. So now I'm a sworn deputy?"

"Yup. Next month, you and three other deputies will go to the Duluth Police Department for a month's training—police school. After school I'll appoint you as a road deputy, no more jail work.

"Jeez, that feels like a promotion," said Luke.

"Yup, a step up in pay and more and different duties. You earned that tonight. You don't get rattled easily, even with gunfire."

"*Mii gwech*, thanks, Sheriff."

Luke put his hat and gun belt in his locker and went in to tell Si all about the evening. He felt himself walking with a swagger, and when he noticed, he stopped and started over again, walking normally.

Si saw him come in. He looked up and said, "Sheriff said you had a little action out there tonight."

"Yeah, I took out one of Billy's tires with a shotgun."

"Well, I put him away for the night in cellblock two. I expect his dad to come by early in the morning to bail him out. He usually does."

"Jeez, how exciting, first time on the road and we had gunfire."

"Last time was about ten years ago when the sheriff was shot in Moose Lake."

"Oooo—must hurt to get shot in the moose lake."

Both laughed at the inane little joke.

The rest of the night passed quietly. At 0600 Luke went home to eat and sleep. He slept until 0845 when a nightmare woke him up for a few minutes. He got up, checked his perimeter, and went back to sleep.

At 0930 his phone rang. Luke picked it up; it was his maa.

"Heard you shot out Billy's tire, almost shot your uncle."

"Nah, only shot the tire—didn't come close to shooting anyone."

"I thought I'd call and get it straight from your horse's mouth."

"Okay, I'm going back to sleep."

"Goodbye, son. Oh, yeah. Your grampa wants to talk to you. Him and his friends want to know what you did in Vietnam."

"Okay. I'll stop by later this afternoon."

"I'll tell him."

That afternoon Luke drove to his grampa's house. He could see him and some other old men sitting in the shade of a tall white pine tree. Luke parked his car and joined them in the shade. There were five of them sitting on chairs and benches in a semicircle.

"*Boozhoo*, shooter man," one of them said. They all laughed.

"Your uncle Besaa said that shotgun woke him up. He thought you were going to shoot him next."

"Nah, they were all pretty drunk and harmless once I took their rifle away."

"Want some tea?" asked his grampa.

After he accepted the cup of hot green tea, one of them asked Luke, "What did you do in the war?"

Luke thought how to answer this question, how to sum up thirteen months in the rice paddies and jungles.

"It was mostly boring; we walked a lot looking for the bad guys. We used to chase them until they caught us," answered Luke. They all smiled at Luke. He continued. "I was in the infantry, we called ourselves grunts."

"Grunts?" one of them asked.

"Yeah, that's the noise you make when you throw a forty-pound pack on your back, buckle on a ten-pound cartridge belt, and put a two-pound helmet on your head. Walking in the rice paddies all day was kinda like walking in that black mud in the swamps.

All of the old men nodded knowingly, they knew that feeling. The black mud of the swamps reminded them of some stories but they let the young man talk.

"I carried an M-fourteen rifle—about twelve pounds—it was a sweet one, and it hit what you were pointing at. It was a seven point six two millimeter, same as a three-zero-eight deer rifle. If you kept it clean it never jammed. I spent many hours taking it apart and scrubbing it with a toothbrush and oil."

"Didn't that oil taste funny?" one of the old men laughed.

"*Gaawiin, gaawiin*, I had two of them, one for my teeth and one for my rifle. I made sure the guys in my squad kept their rifles clean too. The ammo was free; they gave you as much as you wanted to carry. I carried two hundred rounds, most of the other guys carried a hundred.

"Were you in combat every day?" one old man wanted to know.

"I think if one person is shooting at you that makes it combat, but *gaawiin*, I didn't get shot at every day. Still, there was always the tension of knowing you could step on a mine or walk into an ambush at any time. Most of the time it was boring, but when it was exciting, it happened real sudden. Hearing the mortars coming in was pretty scary too. All you can do is just lie there. One time I saw a VC clearly aiming at me with his rifle. I saw the smoke from the barrel and heard the bullet snap by. He missed, but I didn't."

It was quiet for a while among the men sitting in the shade.

"What was the hardest part?" asked Luke's grampa.

Luke took a sip of his tea and thought back to his time in the war: he was seeing the bodies of men he had shot, or stabbed with his bayonet, the crying of the wounded. The coppery smell of human blood, what the inside of a body smelled like. The bravery of his Marines who ran forward when getting shot at, the heat and the rain, the feeling of always being hungry or thirsty.

"I guess the hardest part was loading the dead and wounded Marines on the helicopters after a firefight. It was always confusing, the noise of them big blades spinning above you, the sound

of the chopper engine, the moaning of the wounded, the door
gunner banging away with his machine gun—it was hard to tell
who was what in that confusion. The ones who had been close
to an explosion always were dusted with burnt powder; white
guys looked like black guys. You could hear the thunk-thunk
sounds of enemy bullets hitting the chopper. One time we had
just finished, and as the chopper was lifting off, a surge of blood
came out the door as the bird tilted. The blades turned it into a
mist. All of us were all looking up when the mist hit. I could feel
droplets of blood hitting my face, speckling my glasses."

The old men sat in silence because Luke was done talking.
They could tell by the way he slumped his shoulders and stared
into nowhere.

Luke's grampa got up and went into the house. He came
back out with his pipe bag. He assembled the pipe and filled it
with Prince Albert tobacco he took out from a can. He lit it, had
a couple of puffs and passed it to the next man. At first it was
quiet, then the old men started to talk rapidly in Ojibwe.

Luke didn't know much of the language but he caught
words every now and then, enough to know they were talking
about him. They all smoked the pipe, including Luke.

When the pipe was smoked up, his grampa took it apart
and put it back in his pipe bag. He pulled an eagle feather out,
smudged it with some smoldering sage smoke, and handed it
to Luke.

"This is your feather," his grampa said.

"*Mii gwech, mii gwech,* thank you, Grampa," was all he
could say.

One of the old men asked him, "So you gonna go hunting
Indians tonight?"

"No, no, that was a one-shot deal with Besaa and Billy. I
got to work in the jail until I finish police school in Duluth."

He walked slowly back to his car. He could feel all of them
looking at him, watching him. Luke knew they had accepted

him as *Ogichida*, a warrior. He gave them all a Sawyer wave and drove home to sleep.

The body smell of the man he was grappling with was strong and harsh. Luke spun as the Vietcong knocked his rifle out of his hands. He reached back and drew his Ka-Bar knife. He tried to slash the man's throat, the VC grabbed at his knife arm. Luke drew back and plunged the knife into his stomach.

His knife was buried to the hilt. He quickly pushed the knife in again. The man quit moving, so Luke cut his throat and watched the blood pump out. The smell of blood was everywhere. Luke felt his heart beating at about two hundred beats a minute. His helmet felt like it weighed fifty pounds. He rejoined the patrol. He wanted to brag about his kill but felt too guilty.

CHAPTER SIX

Time passed quickly, Luke thought, but not for the prisoners, only the employees. Luke saw his relatives come and go. And while waiting for police school Luke got to know the rest of the deputies better. He knew which deputies he could trust and which he couldn't. Most of them hadn't earned his trust.

One he could trust was Jim Cuffy. They swapped Marine Corps stories.

"We had a doofus in my platoon in boot camp," Luke said.

"Yeah, we had a couple in my platoon too," Jim replied.

Luke continued, "We were all standing in ranks on the drill field learning the proper way to salute."

"I remember the commands: Hand Salute! That means you snap your right arm up, touching your hat brim, fingers extended and joined, your arm making a forty-five degree angle. Ready Two! means you cut it away smartly to the position of attention."

"Yup, you remembered," said Luke. "Anyway, when the drill instructor gave the command, forty-six arms went up; the boot Marines were making sure they remembered the part about fingers extended and joined.

"The drill instructors walked through the ranks looking, and I heard one guy catch hell for moving his head down to meet his fingers. The instructors pounced, told the recruit to leave his head where it was, and bring the hand up to it. As they were telling him this, recruits noticed every third word was a swear word."

"Yeah, those drill instructors could really swear," added Jim.

"The senior drill instructor was standing right in front of this doofus guy when he said, 'Ready Two!' The doofus smartly raised his left arm and was touching his hat brim on both sides.

"The senior drill instructor looked, then called the junior drill instructors over to look at the doofus guy. He told them to take him inside the duty hut for further, closer instruction," said Luke, ending his story.

"I bet he got thumped," said Jim.

"I bet."

"I heard you're going to police school next week with those three new guys. I went down there about five, six years ago. I'll tell you one of their tricks. Watch for a guy to come up and talk to the instructor. Take note of his description because they'll quiz you later on what the guy looked like."

"Thanks, *mii gwech*, I'll remember that," said Luke.

On a Friday afternoon the sheriff announced the four new men would be going to police school in Duluth. He said they could use one of the squad cars for the daily trip. It was thirty miles one way and Luke was happy he wasn't putting miles on his car.

Everyone left the jail except the new deputies. They were sitting at the kitchen table drinking coffee. Luke walked back to the jail to check in for work, then realized he forgot his coffee cup. He walked back to the kitchen and heard the other deputies talking about him. He stopped in the hall to listen.

"We'll have to teach our blanket ass to read and write next week," said Deputy Bergland. The three of them shared a laugh.

"I'll teach the bow and arrow which end of the pistol the bullet comes out of," said another. They didn't know he had spent thirteen months in combat.

They laughed again.

Luke walked back in the room, which stopped the laughter. He poured a cup of coffee, feeling their eyes on the back of his neck. He turned and smiled at them and walked back to the jail.

"We'll meet here at zero seven thirty," said one of them to his back.

"Ten-four," said Luke.

When Luke got home that night he talked with Carrie about what the white deputies had called him. He told her it felt like they were testing him, pushing to see how hard they could push, waiting to see if he would snap.

The following Monday they met for the drive to Duluth. They had agreed to take turns driving. Luke was scheduled for his turn the following week.

When they got to Duluth, they drove to city hall and parked. The classes were to be held in the basement.

Once inside they began meeting their classmates. Twenty-three were from the Duluth Police Department, four were deputies from St. Louis County, and the four of them were from Carlton County. Luke saw he was the only Anishinaabe in the whole class.

A Duluth police detective introduced himself as one of their instructors and showed them to the classroom. He pointed out the training schedule on the bulletin board. He advised them to check it every morning for possible changes.

He started talking about the life of a police officer and advised them to take notes. He told them a couple of cop stories—some were funny, and some were grim. Luke listened carefully and wrote in his notebook. Already he liked what he was learning. That afternoon an assistant county attorney came in and talked about the law regarding arrests, search and seizure, and preserving evidence.

The days were filled with learning. On one day they were taken to various sites in the city where Duluth police officers were operating radar units to catch speeders. The policeman driving the squad car showed how he parked so that only the radar gun was sticking out.

During one of the classes a man came in the back door, caught the instructor's eye, and approached the front of the class. He leaned in to whisper something to the instructor. This was the trick that fellow Marine Jim Cuffy warned Luke about. Luke studied the man, took detailed notes on what the man looked like. After he was out the rear door the instructor said policemen, including deputies, should be good observers. He then asked them to describe the man who just left. He said they had had a chance to look at him because he was in front of them for two minutes.

The descriptions given were vague—some thought he was carrying a brown sports coat, others remembered a yellow one. They all agreed he had short brown hair but couldn't agree on whether he had a mustache.

When the suggestions died down Luke stood up and read his notes describing the man. "White male, about thirty years old, five foot ten, maybe a hundred and eighty pounds, brown mustache, dragon tattoo on left forearm, gold watch and gold wedding band, brown hair parted on the left side, white shirt with the sleeves rolled up, carrying a yellow sports coat, wearing a wide brown belt, black cuffed pants, brown shoes, gray socks."

The instructor smiled at Luke and told the class they should learn to observe like that deputy. Luke sat down to scattered applause, but none of the deputies from Carlton County were applauding. The described man came back in and stood at the front of the class again. He slowly turned around in front of them, and the class was quick to point out that Luke had missed the anchor tattooed on the man's right forearm. The man said he was from the detective bureau. He then walked over to the instructor's desk and took out a holstered pistol and put it back on his belt. He was right-handed, Luke noted.

The class after that began when the instructor pulled a screen down in front of them; at the rear of the class he set up a slide projector. He then explained what he was doing. He said he was going to show a picture of a traffic scene and told them to look for a license plate in the slide. They got used to reading off the license plate shown.

The instructor explained that he was going to speed it up a bit. He started with the picture being visible for one full second. Next he showed if for half a second, and most of the class could still remember the plate. He kept cutting the time the picture was visible. He then stopped and talked about the retinal after-image. He told them to immediately close their eyes after they saw the picture flash on the screen and to read the license plate off their closed eyelids.

Luke and the others were amazed how well that worked. He had never heard of that before. Then Luke thought back to when he and the sheriff were looking for Billy Wildman: that was how he was able to read license plates that flashed by. Luke thought it was very similar to the way he used to use his eyes when patrolling in the 'Nam.

On another day they were taught how to safely search a potentially armed suspect. First, they learned to tell the suspect to get on his knees, cross his ankles, and lace his fingers together behind the neck. They practiced this method for an entire day. At times he was the designated armed suspect, and other times he was the arresting officer. Luke learned how easy it was to pull someone off balance if they decided to struggle. Luke liked this one because he knew that sometimes he would be the only deputy responding to a call.

They also learned how to search a suspect's car or house. Luke liked the hand-to-hand combat classes; this training built on and added to the training he had received in the Marine Corps. He learned takedowns and come-along holds. He also learned the proper way to handcuff a suspect: behind the back,

back of the hands facing each other. On every ride home he reviewed the notes he had taken that day. Two of the other deputies used the half-hour ride to catch up on their sleep.

Luke liked the three days they spent at the pistol range. The new law enforcement members learned how to shoot and clean their pistols. They also practiced with 12 gauge shotguns. The shooters compared their scores and he smiled when he saw that he outshot his fellow deputies from Carlton County in both pistol and shotgun shooting. It was really quiet on the ride home that day. Luke was happy to report the shooting scores to the sheriff, who told him not to be too hard on his fellow deputies. They hadn't survived thirteen months of combat. Not even close.

Another favorite class was the first aid section; this was all familiar to Luke. He knew CPR already and remembered the U.S. Navy Corpsman mantra: "Stop the bleeding, protect the wound, treat for shock, and if the face is pale, raise the tail, if the face is red, raise the head." He knew he would be the first person at the scene of car crashes, so he really paid attention to the medical professionals who were lecturing that day.

During the question-and-answer period at the end of the class Luke asked if a new Kotex pad could be used as a battle dressing in an emergency situation. Luke's classmates laughed at him. The MD said in his opinion that both were designed to absorb blood, and if the new Kotex were sealed it would remain relatively sterile.

Luke was thinking of the first aid kit he would keep in the trunk of his squad car once he got out on the road. Plastic-wrapped Kotex pads would be in there, along with tape and scissors to cut clothing to get at the wounds—just like the corpsmen he had served with in the 'Nam.

The police school went on for four more weeks and, when he wasn't behind the wheel, Luke continued studying his notes on the ride back to Carlton each evening. He wanted to be ready for the comprehensive written exam that marked the end of their studies.

The test on a Friday morning was long and covered many subjects. Luke was glad he had studied so much because the correct answers jumped out at him on the multiple-choice test.

When the tests were graded Luke found out he was first in the class. His classmates applauded; the Carlton County deputies were silent. A photographer took his picture for the Duluth newspaper.

They got into the car for the ride back to Carlton. It was quiet in the car until Luke swiveled in the front seat and addressed his fellow deputies. "I guess the fucking bow and arrow learned how to read and write pretty quick, eh? Shoot too."

Then, though it didn't seem possible, it got even quieter in the car.

Back at Carlton, the sheriff, Pearl, and Si congratulated him on his position as first in his class.

CHAPTER SEVEN

Luke was now a certified deputy sheriff. He was a road deputy and joined the rotation list for the road patrol. He was assigned a squad car.

On his time off Luke drove the squad car to his maa and dad's house. They were both home and came outside to look at his car. Luke happily showed it off.

Luke's dad asked, "How fast does this car go?"

"I had it up to a hundred and twenty-five miles per hour."

"No shit—that old Ford I used to have would go that fast."

"Dad, the radio inside on the dash travels at the speed of light, a hundred and eighty-six thousand miles per second."

"Go visit your grampa, he kinda missed you."

After visiting with his dad and maa, Luke drove to his grampa's house and showed him his squad car. His grampa thought it was pretty good. The old man told his grandson, "*Weweni nininjanis*," as he was leaving.

Luke stopped at his cousin's house. Niitaawis came out and looked at the car, then Dunkin Black Kettle told him something troubling. "I heard those Cloquet Indians are gonna gang you, beat you up."

"If they try, they'll know they've been in a fight, waking up in the hospital or the cellblock in Carlton," bragged Luke.

"What's worse is they said they were gonna take your badge away and stick it up your ass."

"Then there'll really be a big fight. I can take a beating, but my ass is exit only—that's going too far."

"Just thought I'd tell you what I heard," said Dunkin.

After the visit Luke drove back to Carlton. He had a date with Carrie East that evening.

While eating dinner at a nice place in Duluth, he noticed they spent most of the time looking at each other's eyes. I would like to wake up next to her the rest of my life, Luke thought. They talked about their plans to live together in his little house in Carlton. She could make the drive to her classes in Superior and he could walk to work.

Luke took her to meet his maa and dad. When the two women started cooking together, Luke saw it as a good sign. His dad knew some people from her family in Grand Portage.

Meanwhile Luke was finding it interesting being a road deputy. He investigated crimes and car accidents and hauled drunks to jail. It felt good to talk to Carrie about his shift at work. He didn't get into the gory details of what he was seeing, but she was his antidote to the racism he saw and felt every day. It took the pain away when they talked about such things.

When the war nightmares visited it felt good when she talked softly to him, assuring him he was home and safe. He told her about some of the things he saw in the war in Vietnam. She held him when he felt like sobbing. He never cried.

When they parted for work or school, he counted the hours until he would see her again. He felt like he cared for her, like his maa and dad felt about each other. Luke thought he was feeling what the movies called love.

One night while working in the southern part of the county he got a call from the dispatcher telling him of a car accident at the intersection of Reservation and Brookston Roads. He turned on the red lights on the roof of his squad car. He only used his siren when he was in traffic.

While driving to the scene of the accident, he realized that almost every time something happened on the Reservation he was the one dispatched on the call. He didn't mind; he was dealing with people he knew and no one got beat up when they were arrested.

When Luke got to the scene he used his spotlight to find the wreckage. He found the car: it looked like a crumpled ball of what used to be a car. There was no one around. Luke found where the car left the road and then located where it used the ditch as a ramp to launch though the air. On the north side of the intersection Luke saw where the car had broken a telephone pole off. The stub of the pole was about fifteen feet off the ground. From the paint on the pole Luke determined the car was upside down when it broke the pole. There was a large impact mark where the car landed. It then rolled up on the road where Luke found it.

Luke called the dispatcher on the radio to see if anyone had been brought to the hospital in Cloquet. From the damage he saw to the car, he knew someone must have been hurt in the crash.

He expanded his search for the driver. By this time another deputy, Paul Peterson, had arrived. They began walking along the road looking for the driver.

They couldn't find him, so Luke drove north on Brookston Road. After about five hundred yards Luke's spotlight picked up a human form sitting on the side of the road. He was sitting with his feet toward the ditch as Luke came running up. He was complaining about a stomachache. Luke shined his light down, lifted the man's shirt, and saw he had a cut that started near his belly button then continued around to the small of his back.

The smell of human guts comes back quickly, but no intestines popping out, thought Luke.

The cut was bleeding, so Luke got his first aid kit and used three Kotex pads to cover the wound. He applied tape to hold his crude bandage in place. The man was still complaining about a stomachache. Luke told him to sit still because the ambulance—the meat wagon as they called it—was on the way. Luke covered the man with a blanket while waiting for the ambulance to arrive.

The ambulance arrived and the paramedics saw Luke's bandages and told him that the Kotex had stopped the bleeding. They put the guy on a stretcher and put him in the ambulance. Luke would talk to him after the doctor did his work at the hospital. He called for a hook to remove the car. Both deputies went back to work, and Luke told the dispatcher he had to talk to the man at the hospital as part of his investigation.

When he got to the hospital, the doctor said Luke could see him in few minutes. While waiting, he told Luke the Kotex had stopped the bleeding and wondered where Luke learned it. Luke told him he wasn't sure but he might have invented it. The doctor gave Luke several large compresses so he wouldn't have to use Kotex pads anymore.

Luke went to the injured guy's room. He didn't recognize him but thought he was a Cloquet Indian, someone from the Cloquet part of the Rez. At times there was a rivalry between the two largest communities on the Reservation: the Sawyer Indians thought the ones from Cloquet were all too much like white men and that Cloquet Indians always wished they were Sawyer Indians. The Cloquet Indians thought the Sawyer Indians were too backward, too pagan as their priest told them—didn't look white at all.

When Luke went into the room he asked the man what happened. He said he didn't know but was just going home after being at a party. Luke wrote him a ticket for careless driving but decided against writing him a ticket for leaving the scene of an accident. After his paperwork was done Luke resumed his patrol.

On his day off Luke took Carrie to visit his maa and dad again. Both were home. They visited and laughed. His maa told Carrie some funny stories about Luke when he was a young boy. She also fed them.

Luke's maa asked him when they were going to live together. She could see the bond between the two.

"Last week," said Luke, smiling smugly at her.

Luke noticed his flashbacks were getting farther and farther apart. Maybe because being a deputy took his mind off of the war. He also thought he was fighting a new kind of war—this one was him against crime and racism. Carrie was a big help in his readjusting to civilian life, especially the racism part.

Carrie woke up next to Luke. He was yelling and flailing his arms around, his legs were trying to run. She rolled away until he stopped flailing, then moved back, whispering gently the whole time. She told him this wasn't Vietnam, she asked him if he wanted to talk about his nightmare. He didn't want to talk but felt good that she asked. They hugged and kissed a couple times and both went back to sleep.

CHAPTER EIGHT

After a couple of months on the job, Luke thought the bulk of the work consisted of car accidents and arresting drunks. Of the two, he preferred investigating the accidents.

He got a jolt of adrenaline when he was helping the injured.

Luke wondered if he was an adrenaline junkie. He didn't feel quite right unless there was some excitement going on and he was in the middle of it. The exciting times weren't common but he liked them a lot. A high-speed chase would do it every time.

Luke was running the tapes at the edge of Carlton, the county seat. The tapes were electromechanical devices for measuring the speed of a vehicle passing over them. They were placed on the road exactly ten feet apart with a cable connecting to the device in the squad car. The speed of the cars going by registered on the face of the device. It was a thirty-mile-per-hour zone.

The locals in town knew about the tapes and made sure they were going the legal speed, but once in a while someone would go speeding through.

The alarm went off, Luke looked at the device. The driver was doing fifty-one in a thirty zone. Luke disconnected the cable. He threw it out the window and pulled out after the speeding car.

He had his red lights on. The speeder ignored him. He turned on his siren. The speeder sped up. So did Luke. He got on the radio letting everyone know he had a high-speed chase. He described the car. His speedometer read eighty-five miles per hour. He gave his location and direction of travel.

When Luke radioed the description of the car he used the word CYMBAL: color, year, make, body, and license. He remembered that one from police school. The car he was chasing was a red '64 Chevy two-door, and he wasn't close enough to read the license plates.

The chase continued. They were doing 95 to 105 miles per hour on the two-lane highway. Other cars were pulling over when they saw the chase.

Luke's adrenaline kicked in. Time slowed down for him. The speeding car didn't. His heart was beating faster. They continued toward Duluth. The radio said Duluth squads were waiting. The highway patrol was behind him.

After about eight miles of chasing Luke saw a large cloud of blue-gray smoke coming from the speeder's car. Blew the engine, Luke thought. The chase was over. The speeder slowed up and pulled over to the side of the road. Luke didn't know if he was about to confront just a speeder or an escaping felon. When he got close to the car, the door opened and the driver came running toward Luke. His hands were raised but Luke didn't see a weapon. As the man got close Luke sidestepped him, tripped him, and pushed him to the ground. He got on top and pulled one arm behind him, holding it in place with his knee. He pulled the second arm behind his back and put the handcuffs on him. He got up, then he helped the man up.

The highway patrolman came running over; Luke could tell he was feeling an adrenaline rush too because he was talking fast and taking quick shallow breaths, head and eyes darting around. He began quickly searching the car. He didn't find any contraband or weapons so he searched again.

Luke put the man in the backseat, fastened his seat belt, and got out to talk to the highway patrolman. "Will you call for a hook for the car?" he asked.

"Sure thing. I'm going to search this car again—this guy is dirty. Why else would he be running?"

Luke got in his car and began writing tickets for the offender. He had one each for reckless driving, speeding, revoked driver's license, and disorderly conduct.

"Aha!" yelled the highway patrolman. He had a plastic baggie full of a green substance.

The guy in the backseat said, "Shit."

The highway patrolman came up to Luke's window and gave him the marijuana. He got a whiff of it. Luke added one more charge of possession of a controlled substance.

"I'm going to check the backseat under the carpets, that sandwich bag was under the front-seat carpet."

The state trooper searched some more and found another plastic bag that contained marijuana. He brought that one over to Luke and gave it to him to preserve the chain of evidence.

Luke looked at the man in the backseat of the patrol car. "Now I know why you tried to outrun me."

The Indian male—about twenty-five, long brown hair, brown eyes, wearing a gray sweatshirt, blue jeans, and brown shoes—didn't say a word. He just looked at the floor of the car.

When they got to the jail, Luke turned the prisoner over to Val and began his paperwork. He marked the evidence, sealed it with tape, and locked it in the locker. He wrote out the citations for a man he now knew as Ray Lately of Minneapolis, an enrollee from White Earth. Luke thought he was a mule delivering the marijuana to a dealer in Duluth. While checking with the Bureau of Criminal Apprehension, Luke learned Mr. Lately had an extensive history of drug-related offenses. Lately was also a Marine veteran of Vietnam, but he handled his PTSD differently than Luke did. When he was finished, Luke went home and saw and smelled that Carrie was cooking supper.

He kissed her, hugged her for a long time, then went to take a shower. By the time he was done she had supper on the table.

While eating, Carrie asked, "Were you driving your patrol car real fast on Highway 61 near Nopeming this afternoon?"

"Yeah, I had a chase—a guy didn't want to stop for my red lights and siren."

"Were cars pulling off the road for you?"

"I remember a couple of them near Esko as we flew by."

"One of them was me."

"Oh," he said, wondering where this conversation was going.

Her next question told him where she was going. "Do you have life insurance with your job?"

"Yeah, a ten thousand dollar policy. My maa and dad are the beneficiaries."

"Maybe you should increase it, especially after what I saw this afternoon. You have a dangerous job, Luke Warmwater."

"Good idea, I'll do that tomorrow." He didn't tell her he was going to name her as a beneficiary. A man has to have some secrets.

They spent the evening together, watching TV and planning their future—a future that included children after she graduated from college.

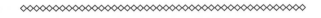

The following night Luke was patrolling the north side of the county. It was a quiet night until about 1243—forty-three minutes after midnight.

"County, one-oh-four, big fight at the truck stop café."

"One-zero-four, county, ten-four, where is the other deputy on this shift?"

"County, one-oh-four, he's tied up with an accident in Barnum, waiting for the meat wagon."

"One-zero-four, county, ten-four, I'll see what I can do at the truck stop."

"County, one-oh-four, be careful."

"One-zero-four, county, always."

Luke quickly drove to the scene. He was using his red lights and siren to clear the road. When he got to the truck stop he parked in front, shut off the siren, but left the red lights on. His spotlight was pointed at the interior of the café.

Luke walked in and saw one, two, three, four, five men fighting, two of them rolling on the floor, three throwing punches and kicking. Three other men were cheering them on. One man was hiding in the kitchen with the waitresses and cook.

Luke slammed his nightstick down hard on the counter. The sudden noise echoed through the small café. It got the fighters' attention. They stopped and looked at Luke. Two of the fighters turned and began coming toward him.

"Hey, look, it's the fucking Indian deputy."

"Let's fuck up that blanket ass."

When they got close, Luke used his nightstick and poked one in the stomach deeply. The man stepped back, gagging, and began vomiting. The second froze when he saw his friend disabled. This gave Luke time to swivel and poke the second one in the stomach. He repeated the first one's actions: backed up, puke exploding out of him.

The rest of the men stopped and waited for Luke's next order. He used his nightstick to point at each of them and told them to sit down on the floor. One by one they obeyed his order. The two who were puking stopped and looked at him with hateful eyes.

Luke sat at the counter, calling them one at a time to stand in front of him and produce identification. He wrote each one a citation for disorderly conduct and told them they would have to pay for the property damage. Then he told them to get in their cars and go home.

As they left, Luke went into the kitchen and talked to the cook. He gave him a list of the men and looked for property damage. There were some broken dishes on the floor and a small piece of glass was broken in the display window. The pies had a sprinkling of window glass on them and were ruined. Luke told the cook to total the damages and split the replacement costs among all nine of them.

◇◇

Luke looked on his job as a deputy as something keeping him from spending all of his time with Carrie. He liked her long black hair, her deep brown eyes. He liked to put his hands under her arms and lift her straight up; it was easy because she only weighed 105 pounds. She was one inch shorter than him. They held hands whenever they walked together.

Deputy Warmwater had just finished the day shift and had walked to his rented house. He was hungry. But first he wanted to take a shower.

When he got out of the shower and was toweling off he thought of what he would make for supper. Damn it, he thought, I don't mind cooking, I made over a thousand C-ration meals in the 'Nam. But he didn't like eating alone.

Carrie had an evening class and he wouldn't see her until later that night.

He had eaten everything on the truck stop menu at least once. Whenever he ate there he ran into two kinds of people. There were those who knew he was a deputy and acted all kiss-assy with him, offering to pay for his meal. But Luke knew there was no such thing as a favor granted without one being expected in return. He preferred to pay for his own meals. Then there were the people who didn't know him; they just saw an Indian, someone to stay away from. Of those people, he thought, am I so loathsome they won't even look at me?

Whenever he ate at his maa's house he didn't feel any of those things, he just felt like he was home again. But he knew eating there meant he was taking scarce food from the family.

When he was looking in the cupboard the phone rang. Luke picked up the phone and said, "Hello?"

"*Boozhoo*, Luke, this is your maa."

"*Boozhoo*, Maa, I just got home."

"I know, I just talked to the jailer."

"*Aaniin ezhi chigeyan?*"

"Your dad, he took a load of wood to town and he's drinking up the check. These kids are hungry. Go find him," she continued, "get some of that money so I can feed these kids."

"Aw, Maa, I just spent twelve hours in that squad car—call the night deputy."

"These are your brothers and sisters," she said, ending the discussion.

"Okay, I'll take a look around."

"*Mii gwech, Ningwis.*"

He put his uniform back on and pulled on his boots. Buckling his gun belt around his skinny *Shinnob* hips, Luke wrote a note so Carrie would know where he was. He looked into the large mirror before walking outside and locking his door—yup, looked like a deputy. Luke walked to the sheriff's office one block away.

Upon his arrival, Luke rang the bell and waited for the jailer to open the steel barred door.

As the heavy door swung open, Val smiled at Luke and said, "Did you arrest yourself?"

"No, no. My maa just called and said my dad was raising hell again."

"I thought something was up when she called here looking for you."

"Yup, and now I'm the one who has to go looking for my dad."

"I'll make a note in the log. Doesn't your dad like to drink at Timber's Inn in Cloquet?"

"I think he likes to drink anywhere," Luke said, heading out the back door for his squad car. He clicked his seat belt and checked the lights, the siren, and the radio. While the radio was warming up, Luke checked the shotgun. Yup, still loaded the way he had left it a half hour earlier. He also checked the flashlight, then picked up the microphone. "One-zero-three, one-zero-six, one-zero-four is ten-eight," Luke told the two deputies currently on duty.

"One-oh-four, one-oh-six, where you headed?"

"One-zero-six, I'm going to the Rez, going to check on a few things."

"One-oh-four, one-oh-three, can't get enough of this job, eh? Be careful around those bow and arrows."

"Ten-four." Luke didn't respond to the racial slur.

Luke drove to Sawyer and checked his dad's usual stops. He didn't see the familiar red pulp truck. No one had seen the truck since it had left for town. Luke headed to Cloquet on the Big Lake Road, might snag up a speeder on the way.

He drove north on Reservation Road and continued looking for his dad's logging truck. He didn't see it anywhere, so he decided to head for Cloquet to see if it was parked near one of the bars in town.

He drove by Timber's Inn, and a quick scan revealed his dad's truck near the back of the lot, almost in the shadows. He drove over and parked behind it. He peeked in the cab and didn't see anyone asleep on the wide front seat. He opened the hood and took off the distributor cap; no one would be driving that truck tonight.

Luke drove over by the front door and parked his squad car. He took the steps two at a time, stepped inside, and just stood by the front door. The smell of stale beer and cigarette smoke washed over him.

Hank Williams's sad song on the jukebox ended as he walked in. He looked around the bar. The drinkers stared back at him, so did the bartender. It was unusual to see a deputy in uniform in the bar.

Luke saw his dad at the end of the bar. He was alone and staring into his half-empty glass. Luke walked down and stood next to him. He could feel everyone's eyes on him. He leaned down and said, "Dad, let's go outside, I need to talk to you."

His dad ignored him. Luke said it in a slightly louder voice, "Dad, let's go outside."

His dad looked up at him and shook his head no. Luke tried again, "C'mon Dad, let's go outside."

His dad swiveled on his barstool and said in a slurred voice, "No fucking son of mine is telling me what to do."

"I'm not telling, Dad, I'm asking you to come outside with me."

"Get the fuck out of here, leave me alone."

"I can't do that, Dad, I want you to come outside with me."

The drunk swung a mighty backhand at his son. Luke had plenty of experience in ducking those backhands so he just stepped back out of the way. It was no longer a family thing—it suddenly became a law enforcement matter. You can't swing at a uniformed deputy without facing the consequences.

His dad almost fell off the stool when he missed. Before he could do anything else Luke grabbed him in a come-along hold. He bent his dad's thumb backward, moved his arm inside of his dad's arm, and pulled him off the barstool. He spun him in a couple of circles to disorient him and began toe walking him to the front door. His dad was still trying to hit him, but he was way off balance and couldn't punch across his body to hit Luke.

He was six inches taller than his dad, probably outweighed him by sixty pounds, and was twenty years younger, so Luke was in control. The bar patrons and the bartender were watching this unequal struggle.

While going down the front stairs his dad tripped him and both men fell down; Luke hung on to his come-along hold as they rolled down the steps. If this was anyone else he would have hurt him and ended the fight, but Luke didn't want to hurt his dad.

All the people in the bar except the bartender came out to watch the two Indians, father and son, rolling around in the gravel of the parking lot.

Luke was able to get one handcuff around his dad's wrist, and after some struggling he tried placing the second handcuff on. The damn thing was double locked, Luke quickly realized. That meant he needed a handcuff key to be able to use it. The nearest key was on his key ring inside the ignition of the idling squad car. Luke wrestled his dad toward the car, who was trying to punch him in the face or head along the way. He ducked his dad's fist, then ducked again as the heavy steel handcuff came swinging by.

When they got near the squad car Luke was able to reach in and take the keys out of the ignition. Still dodging punches, he rode his dad to the ground. He fumbled around and finally got the handcuff unlocked, then he helped his dad stand up and walked him to the backseat of the car.

The crowd of watchers was either cheering or booing.

His dad began struggling in the backseat. He was trying to head-butt Luke, then he lay on his back and began kicking at him with both feet. Luke just stayed out of the way. When his dad started kicking at the squad car windows Luke had to do something. He pushed his dad down on the floor between the front- and backseat and lay on top of him. There, it was all under control again. He had his dad contained so he couldn't hurt himself or others. Both were on the floor in the backseat trying to catch their breath. Luke got up when his dad seemed to be resting.

He got out of the backseat and into the front seat. He was just putting the keys in the ignition when his dad began kicking the windows again.

Luke got back out of the car, pushed his dad to the floor, and lay on top of him again. Luke was in control but couldn't drive from the backseat.

Luke looked at the crowd of onlookers. He was looking for the soberest one. When he saw a guy he thought might qualify he said in his loud Marine Corps voice, "You—I want you to help me. Drive this squad car to the county jail."

The man stepped forward and said, "Really? All right! I never drove one of these before—always wanted to but never had the chance. How do you drive it?"

"Just drive it like a regular car," Luke told his citizen-helper.

"Where's the red lights and siren?"

"You don't need them," Luke said. "Just drive."

The citizen-helper was flipping switches and the siren came on. In the evening shadows Luke could see the red lights sweeping the parking lot. His dad seemed activated by the siren and began struggling again.

His helper drove the squad car out of the parking lot and onto Big Lake Road, lights flashing and siren blaring. He was headed in the general direction of the county jail so Luke didn't say anything.

The citizen-helper began talking on the radio. "Hello, hello, anyone out there?"

"Go ahead, county squad."

"I'm helping this deputy, he's in the backseat with the prisoner."

"Ten-four, where are you going?"

"I'm going to the county jail."

"Ten-four, turn off that siren."

"I don't know which switch it is." The helper was again flipping switches.

"Just drive to Carlton then," the dispatcher advised.

"Okay, Roger Wilco. Goodbye."

Luke heard the ominous click of the electric shotgun lock.

He raised his head above the passenger seat and realized he was staring into the muzzle of his own 12 gauge shotgun. When the lock popped open the shotgun fell back and was leaning against the passenger seat. He ducked out of the line of fire and told his helper to stop the car.

The driver complied. Luke got out of the backseat and got his helper out of the front seat. Luke told him he was under arrest for disorderly conduct. Luke dug out his extra handcuffs and put his helper in the backseat on top of his dad.

He turned off the red lights and siren, put the shotgun back in the lock. He picked up his microphone and said, "One-zero-four, I'm ten-eight with two ten-fifteens, ETA Carlton about four minutes."

"Ten-four," said the dispatcher.

When Luke got to the jail he took his two prisoners inside and turned them over to the jailer. The jailer removed the handcuffs and put the prisoners in the cellblock. He smiled as he handed Luke his handcuffs.

"I'll drop the charges against them in the morning," Luke told the jailer.

Luke walked home and changed clothes. He got into his own car and drove to Sawyer. He picked up his maa and drove her to town, loaned her some money so she could buy groceries. No hungry kids on my watch, Luke thought. He drove home afterward and told Carrie about his evening. She applied bandages to his scraped elbows. He explained to her how hard it was to fight with someone without hurting them.

CHAPTER NINE

On his evenings off he and Carrie went out to eat or to the movies. Luke decided not to drink alcohol when he was working in law enforcement. For one thing he was subject to a recall to duty depending on the nature of the emergency. And when he was working in the jail he noticed that alcohol was involved in most of prisoners' problems.

One evening he took Carrie to eat with his family in Sawyer. They shopped for food together at a big grocery store in Duluth. Luke thought he and Carrie were acting like a married couple or something. She went to school and he worked, but every minute of their free time was spent together. She enjoyed living with Luke in Carlton; she was always touching him somehow. Luke was having serious thoughts about their life together. They talked about raising a family, they laughed frequently and at the same time. Luke thought she would be the perfect woman if she just smoked unfiltered Camels and hated liver and onions like he did.

He enjoyed telling her what he was learning as a deputy. She shared what she was learning in college. As an Anishinaabe woman she tried to blunt the blatant racism Luke was facing every day.

Luke's family in Sawyer liked Carrie because she got along with everyone there. Yup, she looked like a keeper.

On one of their weekends off Luke cleared it with his office to let them know he would be out of town until Sunday evening. They drove her car up Highway 61 along the north shore of Lake Superior.

They stopped for a picnic lunch at a wayside just north of Silver Bay. After eating they climbed the trail to the Pali, as the palisade was called. Once on top they went to the edge and looked down at Lake Superior. It looked to be at least a hundred yards out to the blue and green waves rolling in. They enjoyed their time together there, standing in the constant wind.

The two were on their way to the Grand Portage Reservation to meet her family. They got a motel room just outside of Grand Marais because Carrie said it was crowded at her parents' house.

When they arrived in Grand Portage it was suppertime at the house. Chairs and dishes were pushed together to make room for them. They ate and visited, played cards and visited some more. The word got out that Carrie was back in town and relatives kept coming by to see her and her new boyfriend.

Luke and Carrie had a tiring drive back to their motel. They slept in the strange-to-them bed and got up to go back to Portage for more visiting.

About noon they headed south. Luke thought he must have met about fifty people, including the kids. He was hoping there wasn't going to be a quiz on their names.

Once back in Carlton Luke called the office to let them know he was back and would be at home.

The next morning Luke woke up and got dressed. He made his familiar walk to the jail to begin his shift. Carrie got up and got ready for her classes at the university in Superior. She was close to graduating with a degree in biology.

He stopped by to talk to the jailer and checked his equipment. He then went outside and checked his squad car. It was cold—below zero, and with the cold there was a surprise on his car. The women staying in the cell on the second floor had tossed four used tampons onto the hood of his car, where they had frozen. After removing these, Luke waved at the women and drove away laughing.

His first goal was the truck stop for coffee. When he was there, the owner, Pete Peterson, told him the people who were fighting had all paid their share of damages. He thanked Luke for doing his duty, said he was brave to take on nine men. Luke explained there were only nine of them. He and Pete had gone to school together. Luke said most of them didn't really want to fight with a deputy, not a man who carried a big stick. He had simply taken out the two biggest and loudest ones—the ones that posed a threat.

As he was leaving he told Pete he would be back later in the evening with his pretty bride-to-be. Pete told him what was on the menu for the evening meal and said he wanted to meet her.

About halfway through his meal with Carrie that evening, Luke saw what he thought was his cousin's car pull into the parking lot. The car was a '65 GTO, and his cousin Paul was really proud of that fast car.

"Paul Ernest Wog, what brings you to these parts?" asked Luke when his cousin walked in. "Did you come to eat?"

"I was supposed to meet my brother but he probably got tired of waiting. Our classes ran long today. We were learning some new moves at the dojo—that means gym for those of you who don't study karate."

"That sounds like a good workout."

"Want to see some of my new kata?"

"I don't think there's enough room around here. Don't you guys jump around quite a bit?"

"Karate is all about discipline and self-control, so I can show you without breaking anything in here."

"Go ahead, you know you want to."

Paul assumed a stance and began rapidly punching an imaginary opponent. He tried different kinds of punches. Then he threw a couple of kicks into the mix.

Luke and Carrie both gave him a few handclaps when he was done. He looked smug.

"I'm going to the bar next door, call my brother to see what happened," said Paul.

"Okay, see you around then," said Luke as he and Carrie continued eating their meal.

Just as she was about to ask, Luke answered her, "No, not interested in learning karate." Both smiled because they were talking to each other without words.

As they were walking out to their car, a man came running out of the bar.

"Deputy, better go check on your cousin."

Luke walked quickly to the bar. The familiar smells of a beer joint greeted him when he walked in. He didn't see anything unusual: a row of men standing at the bar, some sitting on barstools. A country-western song on the jukebox competed with a fishing show on TV.

Luke saw his cousin on the floor curled into an almost-fetal position. No one at the bar was looking at him. Luke walked over and stared down at Paul. There was a large red mark on the left side of his face. He looked groggy but was conscious.

Luke said, "Paul E. Wog, what the hell happened to you?"

"Don't know, was just showing the guys here what I learned. Someone sucker punched me."

"Who was it?" asked Luke.

"Don't know, it all happened so fast."

"Come on, get up, I'll walk you to your car."

"Thanks, cuz."

After making sure he could drive okay Luke returned to where Carrie was waiting for him. He got into the car. He could hear her silently asking what had happened.

"I guess someone wasn't impressed with his karate moves. Maybe they felt threatened when he was punching too close. Someone gave him a lesson in sucker punches. He'll be okay."

They drove home. Carrie had an evening class so Luke said he would just wait for her at home. She left and he sat down on his chair and was going to turn on the TV when the flashback hit.

<><><><><><><><><><><><><><><><><><><><><><><><><><><><><><><>

Luke ran to the helicopter. It was the one they called HUS—an H-34 in Marine Corps talk. HUS, as in, "Hey, give me a HUS over here. I need ammo/water/food."

He was catching a ride back to An Hoa from Da Nang. He was at the air base to get his pay records straightened out and to see the eye doctor. He ordered two pair of glasses—one with clear lenses and one with tinted green lenses. He only had one pair, and they looked funny because one lens was tinted a different shade of green. He had broken his glasses after diving to the ground once when the VC started shooting at him. The glasses had been in the lower pocket of his jungle jacket, between his body and the ground.

Going back to Da Nang Air Base was a nice escape from the war, a break from the constant patrolling in the bush when the VC rockets weren't coming in.

He went to the big PX where he got white socks for everyone in his squad. Luke was trying to prevent immersion foot, a common malady for the grunts splashing through the rice paddies. He also got foot powder and moleskin for the blisters, along with writing gear, candles, and candy. He was carrying a sandbag full of goodies.

The motor roared loud as the HUS struggled to get off the ground. The inside of the helicopter was packed with small arms ammo, cases of frags, and mortar shells. He found a seat and was staring straight ahead at the stacked boxes of frag grenades.

The whop-whop sound of the helicopter blades could be heard everywhere.

They quit climbing at about two thousand feet and headed south to An Hoa. Suddenly the door gunner began shooting his M60 down toward the ground, the floor under him was littered with brass and links from his machine gun ammo. The sound of the gun gave Luke a jolt of adrenaline. He debated whether he should go to the door and help the gunner who was still shooting. Two grunts were closer and they began banging away with their M14 rifles. Luke stayed put but was still buzzing.

He was looking at the floor. He heard a loud scream and saw the door gunner fall. Once again time was altered: seemingly in slow motion the door gunner quit shooting and grabbed at his right thigh. The grunts near him eased him to the floor and cut his pants leg off and put bandages on the entrance and exit wounds. They pulled him away from the open door. The bullet had missed the big artery in his leg. One grunt jumped behind the machine gun and began firing toward the ground. The other grunt stayed with the wounded gunner.

Luke felt a thump under his left foot. He was staring at the floor when he felt the impact of a bullet. A slit opened up in the aluminum floor between his feet. Luke looked up to find where the bullet had exited through the roof. He couldn't see any holes. An icy hand gripped his heart when he saw the bullet hole in the side of a case of frags right in front of him. Sergeant Warmwater examined the box of frags. One frag had a hole in the black cardboard tube. Luke carefully lifted the grenade out of tube and slowly pulled the tape holding the lid on the case. When it was loose he lifted the grenade out. The bullet had plowed through the side of the grenade. Luke could see a groove through the C-4 explosive and see the blasting cap. The grunt with the wounded door gunner was watching him. Luke showed him the groove in the grenade. The grunt nodded knowingly. Luke slowly walked to the open window and threw the grenade out of the helicopter. Now *he didn't care where it exploded. Luke shouldered another load of survivor guilt.*

Luke came back to the world. He was still sitting on the couch in his living room. He looked at the floor: no holes, no brass or links, no blood. Although he knew he was alone he still looked around the room to see if anyone had seen him take his trip back to Vietnam. He was glad no one was there with him. Another one to tell Carrie about when she came home.

When Carrie got back he told her about the flashback. She held him with her eyes and arms.

The next afternoon Luke was patrolling in the southern part of the county. It was a quiet Sunday and most businesses were closed.

As he came through the little town of Mahtowa he saw a car parked behind the only bar in town, the Elmwood Inn. It wasn't the car used by the owner when he came in on Sundays to clean up—fact is, he didn't drive a car to work, and he drove a red pickup truck.

Luke got on the radio and told the dispatcher he was getting out of his squad car to check on a suspicious vehicle behind the bar in Mahtowa.

The dispatcher asked if he should roll a backup squad to the bar. Luke said that sounded like a good idea. He parked his squad car behind the suspicious car. He felt the hood of the car: it was cold, indicating it had been parked there for a while. He wrote down the description of the car, including the license-plate number. Luke quietly looked at the back of the bar. There were no signs of forced entry, both doors and windows looked secure.

He searched the perimeter of the building, once again the windows looked secure. He came to the front door and tried opening it. The door swung open and Luke stepped back, drawing his pistol at the same time. He listened, still quiet. He thought he heard someone inside breathing—sounded like he was asleep. Luke quietly walked into the dance hall part of the building after making sure no one was hiding behind the bar.

There was a man sleeping on a cot on the bandstand. A nearby table showed two different kinds of cigarette butts in the ashtray, two coffee cups too. Luke thought there was another person in the building.

He looked into the women's bathroom. Empty. Deputy Warmwater entered the men's bathroom. He saw feet and legs under the first stall door and kicked it in. The man inside was shocked to be looking up at the wrong end of Luke's pistol.

Luke told the man to stand up and face away from him.

In a shaky voice the man asked for permission to wipe. Luke told him to do it but to move slowly. He told the man to step back and pull up his pants. Once Luke searched him he took him in the other room and told him to wake up his friend. The man walked over and shook the sleeping man's shoulder. Keeping his pistol pointed at both of them, Luke asked, "Who are you and what are you doing in a closed bar?

The first man answered, "I'm John Neimi from Barnum and we're here guarding the presents." He pointed to a pile of gaily wrapped gift boxes of various sizes. "This is my brother, Pete. His daughter is getting married here this evening and everyone delivered their presents already. We've been here since closing time last night."

The second man was nodding his head up and down in agreement.

After looking at their driver's licenses Luke holstered his pistol. He advised them to let the sheriff's office know if they were ever going to guard something in a closed bar again.

John smiled and said, "Pete's only got one daughter."

Luke accepted the coffee Pete offered and walked over to use the bar phone to cancel the alert. The dispatcher said the northern shift deputy was tied up investigating a car accident and that he had called a deputy at home to respond. Deputy Bergland was coming from Moose Lake to back him up. It was less than ten miles away.

Luke visited with the two guards while waiting for his fellow deputy. After about a half hour Luke decided he'd better get back on patrol. It didn't look like Bergland was going to show up.

Carrie laughed when he told her of his day's adventures. She said, "Did he really ask if he could wipe his butt?"

"Gospel truth," said Luke.

The next week Carrie was reading the Pine Knot, the local weekly newspaper. She handed Luke the newspaper and said, "Are you Deputy Bergland?"

Luke read the newspaper until he came to the Letters to the Editor section. He found a letter written by the chief deputy praising Deputy Bergland for searching the bar and finding the two men guarding wedding presents. In the letter, Deputy Bergland was cited for his bravery and his devotion to duty. The letter closed with the chief deputy saying he was proud to work with a man of such a courageous nature, such a brave man. Luke was snorting by the time he finished reading.

"Why did they leave you out of the story?" asked Carrie.

"I don't know. I'll talk to the sheriff about this when he comes back from that FBI school in Quantico, Virginia.

Luke went back to work, and the following week the sheriff came back from Virginia. Luke went to his office armed with the newspaper.

"I know what you're going to say, said the sheriff. "I saw this and talked to the chief deputy last night. He realizes he made a mistake by writing that letter about the Elmwood Inn matter. He said he'll never do it again."

"This is just one example of how things aren't working out here," said Luke. "After two years of working with them, some of the deputies still call me 'blanket ass' or 'our Indian'. What are you going to do about this letter?" asked Luke.

"Deputy Bergland got two weeks off without pay for his part in that damned letter," said Sheriff Johnson. "The chief deputy will pay a fine too. I'll make it up to you after the next election, I promise you," he said.

"Don't bother, I doubt I'll be here after the next election."

"That will be your decision, of course, but I wish you would stay," said the sheriff. "We're slowly making some progress against racism."

"Too slow for me," said Luke.

"Please tell me you'll stay another year," said the sheriff.

"I guess we'll see, won't we?" replied Luke.

Luke asked for five vacation days that coincided with Carrie's days off from school. The sheriff immediately approved it.

Earlier in the week Luke had received a letter from a friend who had stayed in the Marine Corps. He was hospitalized at Great Lakes Naval Hospital in North Chicago, Illinois. Luke wrote back and told him he would come down there and visit him.

CHAPTER TEN

Luke and Carrie drove to Minneapolis, where they visited Luke's sister Suzy.

She welcomed them into her apartment. "I got coffee or tea and I have some sandwiches for you," said Suzy.

"Good, I could eat the north end of a south-walking caribou," replied Luke.

"As you're driving through Bariboo," answered Suzy, completing his rhyme.

When they sat at the kitchen table Luke said, "Suze, this is my bride-to-be, my new old lady, Carrie East."

"And last old lady," Carrie added.

"I'm glad to meet you. My maa told me so much about you."

"I'm glad to meet you too—you're the first of Luke's sisters I've met. He's always talking about his sisters."

"He was probably lying through his teeth."

"No, he was only saying good things."

"I'm gonna call a couple of my sisters because they wanted to meet you too. They live real close so they'll be over."

"Uh-oh, this sounds like a hen party, Suze. Call Gary and see if our cuz wants to go play pool," said Luke.

Suze called Gary, spoke and laughed a couple of minutes, and told Luke, "Yeah, he said pick him up, he's still giving pool lessons."

Luke picked up Gary and they went to the pool hall where Gary worked.

Gary racked the balls for a game of eight ball. Luke won the first game and Gary ran the table the next four games. Gary was indeed giving pool lessons; Luke was glad they weren't betting. They laughed and lied and played pool for the next couple of hours. Luke thought the hen party was about over so he gave Gary a ride back to apartment with promises of pool games and visiting the next time he was in town.

The warm feelings Luke felt when he walked into his sister's apartment told him the visit had gone well. Luke and Carrie got into his car to continue the trip to North Chicago. They spent the night in a motel in Wisconsin Dells and got up in the morning, ate breakfast, and continued their trip south.

Luke could tell the visit between Carrie and his sisters had been a success. She was telling him about their plans for the next get-together.

They got a motel room in North Chicago and Luke told Carrie he wanted to visit his friend alone. He didn't want to expose her to the debris of war he was sure he would see on the orthopedic ward. She dropped him off at the hospital after agreeing to meet in a couple of hours. She was going to a shopping mall, maybe a Goodwill store too.

Luke walked into the hospital and went to the information desk and learned his friend's location. He took the elevator to the orthopedic ward and checked at the nurses station, where they pointed to his friend's bed.

The ward was a huge room with beds alongside both walls. It must have held twenty-five to thirty patients. He saw his friend waving from halfway down the right side.

Luke didn't really want to look at the patients on his walk to his friend's bed, but he did anyway. Some patients were missing a leg, or both legs; others were wearing plaster casts. Corpsmen were moving from bed to bed caring for their patients.

Luke shook hands with his friend and sat down in the chair next to his bed. He asked the obvious question: "What the hell happened to you?"

"We were sweeping through a village just east of An Hoa. You wouldn't recognize that place. They got a whole Marine regiment there now. It was just a company-sized perimeter when we were there, remember?"

"Yeah, I remember that place, those spooky, scary mountains just to the west of An Hoa," Luke said.

"They got grunts on top of all of those mountains now, choppers keep them resupplied—they can see into the valleys, always calling in artillery or air strikes on the VC."

"Remember that mine I was standing on when we went up one of those mountains?" asked Luke.

"Yeah, you couldn't move because you didn't know if it was a pressure or pressure-release kind of firing chain."

"I remember you were taking pictures of me as I was standing there."

"I was going to catch the explosion if you moved the wrong way. Glad it didn't go off."

"I talked to the engineer that disarmed it, said it was a Chicom left over from when the French were fighting there. He said somehow water got inside and got the black powder all wet."

"Like I said, I'm glad it didn't go off."

"Me too. By the way, what the hell happened to you?"

"Someone was blowing up bunkers and used forty pounds of C-4. The blast was loud and for some reason I was lying on my back. Something big hit my legs. I got a compound fracture on the right one, simple fracture on the left."

"Do you know what hit you?" asked Luke.

"I think it was a chunk of those railroad tracks. Remember how the VC used to tear up the railroad to use those tracks?"

"Yeah, I remember they heated then bent them into a U-shape for their bunkers—made a strong roof. Did you serve with anyone from our old company?"

"No, all new Marines. They fought pretty well when the enemy would show themselves."

"I kind of miss that camaraderie we had."

Luke told his friend of his job as a deputy on the Rez in northern Minnesota. He told him the unvarnished truth.

"Jeez, I wouldn't work there under those conditions."

"The white people hate me because I'm a fucking Indian, the Indians hate me because I'm a fucking pig," said Luke.

"What you gonna do about it?"

"I thought I'd look around here, see if anyone needs an experienced lawman."

"I thought of getting out of the Crotch when my legs heal, thought about being a cop too."

"It has some exciting moments." Luke told his friend about the time he shot out a tire on a high-speed chase.

"Did you want to shoot the driver too?"

"Yeah, thought about it, then remembered this wasn't Vietnam." Luke then shared some of his flashbacks and nightmares about the war.

"I get them sometimes, usually about people I killed."

"Mine seem to be getting smaller, less intense as time goes on," Luke said. He felt like a counselor.

"Maybe there will come a time when you go for long periods without those episodes?"

"Sometimes I don't know if I'm actually remembering something or just making it up as I go along," confessed Luke.

"Who cares—it gets your heart pumping fast either way, doesn't it?"

"Yeah, I got a good woman who holds me and brings me back."

"Good. Lucky you."

Just then Carrie came walking down the aisle looking for Luke. He was surprised to see her there early. He was supposed to meet her in the parking lot in another hour.

"Don't try to shield me from the effects of war," she said. "I see them in you every time you have a flashback or nightmare."

"Yeah, I had doubts about trying that, by coming to the ward alone."

"Introduce me to your friend then."

"Carrie, this is my friend, Sergeant Jim Croyle. His war name was Jim Crow."

"Yeah, now they call me Jimbo and I don't like it," he said, smiling and reaching his hand out to shake hers.

"Okay, mind if I just call you 'Jim'?"

"Yeah, that's what my maw called me—never known her to lie."

The two continued visiting with the wounded Marine until it was time for them to leave. Just for a little while Luke felt the camaraderie he used to have when he was with the Marines in Vietnam.

That evening in their motel room Luke was reading the local newspaper when he noticed a city of Waukegan advertisement for police officers. He showed Carrie the ad and said, "Would you like to live here? Won't your credits transfer?"

"I don't know," she answered, "I'd have to check on that when we get back home."

"I'm going to stop by there tomorrow—bet they'd like an experienced law enforcement officer quicker than a rookie," he said.

They went to sleep. She was thinking of the big changes coming into their shared lives.

The next morning Luke went to the Waukegan Police Department and asked to speak to the recruiter. He was directed to Sergeant Nelson's office down the hall.

Luke knocked on the door. The voice inside said, "C'mon in."

Luke said, "I'm Luke Warmwater, currently a deputy from Carlton County, Minnesota. I see you're looking for patrolmen." He handed the recruiting sergeant a copy of his résumé.

"Have a seat and let me look at this," responded the sergeant. "Ah, I see you've been on the road a bit over two years and completed school at the Duluth Police Department. We just need you to take a few tests and we'll put you on the hiring list for a background check. One of the tests is the Minnesota Multiphasic Personality Inventory—the MMPI. That one will be reviewed by our shrinks."

"Okay, when can I do those tests?"

"This afternoon, if you're free. Oh, I see you were a Marine. So was I—Seventh Marines in Operation Starlite."

"I was with India Company, Third Battalion, Ninth Marines. We were at An Hoa."

That afternoon Luke took the physical agility test and the MMPI.

Sergeant Nelson said, "Everything looks in order. You'll be hearing from us."

"Thanks. I'm always glad to meet another Marine that was in-country."

"I know what you mean—there are a dozen of us in the department, most are in the Patrol Division, night shift."

"That's certainly good to hear, thanks."

"You bet."

Luke walked out of the building, inside he felt like jumping up in the air and clicking his heels but then remembered he didn't do that kind of shit.

Carrie could tell by his walk that it was good news.

They headed north, back to Minnesota. The song "Proud Mary" sang to them on the car radio at one point. Luke nodded his head as they were rolling down the highway; Carrie smiled at her man. She said, "I'll remember this trip the rest of my life."

Luke smiled back at her.

When they got back to Minnesota, Luke returned to road patrol. He felt a certain coolness from his fellow deputies, even from those he felt he could trust. He continued fighting crime but didn't feel the same about it as before—he was just marking time.

Luke and Carrie talked late into the night about how things changed once that letter came out in the newspaper.

Both thought the challenges of a job in Waukegan justified the move. She would transfer her college credits to a nearby university. Carrie said she would call her parents and let them know they were taking their happiness to Waukegan, Illinois.

Luke and Carrie went to Sawyer and talked with his parents about the new opportunity in Waukegan.

"It has been a hard two years on you, hasn't it, son?" asked Luke's maa.

"Yeah, one consolation is Indians don't get beat up by the deputies as much as they did before," Luke said. "I had a hard time fitting in either world, white or Anishinaabe," he continued. "I'm just waiting for a letter from the Waukegan Police Department to let me know if and when I'll start working down there."

"And you say the money is twice what you're getting here?" his maa asked.

"Yeah, and only forty hours a week instead of seventy-two like they work here," answered Luke.

"You should've looked into that job last year," his dad said.

"I didn't know about it until I visited my old Marine buddy at Great Lakes Naval Hospital."

Luke and Carrie went home. Luke checked the mail and found a letter from the Waukegan Police Department.

He walked in and handed the letter to Carrie.

She opened it and read it, then said, "They want you—can you start in ten days?"

"Yeah, I think we can do that."

They hugged.

The next day Luke went to tell the sheriff he was leaving for a job in the Waukegan Police Department.

The sheriff invited him into his office. "I'm sorry to hear that, Luke."

"They pay twice as much as you pay me. A health insurance plan is one of the benefits. They work a forty-hour week too," said Luke.

"I think you helped improve race relations around here."

"I didn't know that was in my job description" said Luke.

"You can have the rest of the time off to make the move then. I got something for you." With that, the sheriff unlocked a door on his desk and continued, "I got a little going away present for you."

He handed Luke a beautiful stainless steel .38 caliber revolver.

"This is called a Chief's Special, I got wadcutter bullets in there now."

"Thanks, Sheriff—I almost said *mii gwech* to you."

"I heard the police officers in the big city always carry a backup gun."

The next week went by fast; Luke and Carrie were sorting out what would go and what they could give away. Luke borrowed a pickup to carry the furniture they were giving away. He took it to Sawyer and it was gone in just a couple of hours.

Carrie and Luke spent hours visiting his close relatives in Sawyer. They spent most of the time with his parents and grandparents.

One night his maa had a feast for Luke and Carrie. The young couple was given many presents from his relatives. When looking through their pile of presents Carrie found a layette set wrapped inside a blanket. Someone was thinking ahead to the future for them.

The next morning Luke was packing the rest of their stuff. Carrie said she had to go to UW–Superior to pick up her transcript because the university in Illinois would accept her credits. He told her he would finish up with all of the packing.

Luke had everything in boxes and bags except the coffeepot and cups. A state highway patrol car pulled up in front of the house. Luke looked out the window and tensed up. A highway patrol trooper came walking up to the front door. This doesn't look good, Luke thought. He invited the trooper in and poured two cups of coffee. They sat at the kitchen table.

The trooper said, "I got bad news for you, Luke."

Because of the way he was moving his eyes around and clearing his throat, Luke knew it was really bad.

They sat at the kitchen table while the trooper explained, "There was a crash on Highway Sixty-One, just west of Nopeming."

Oh, no, Luke thought, which one of my family is dead?

"It was your woman, Carrie. She had her signal on and was turning into a gas station. A logging truck came over the hill and couldn't stop in time. He pushed Carrie's car through a guardrail and into a stand of Norway pines. The car caught fire and the logging truck driver died when he went through the windshield."

Luke sat in the chair, his face was frozen like a Minnesota lake in January.

"Is there anything I can do for you?"

"No, there is nothing."

Luke sat in the silence.

The highway patrolman left. He was glad to have finished up his grisly duty.

Luke called his maa and dad and then told them of her death. On the phone he could hear his maa crying and his dad swearing. He called Carrie's mother in Grand Portage, he explained why he wouldn't be at the funeral. She understood his reason.

He went to the funeral anyway.

He wanted to remember Carrie being alive instead of forever lying in the long gray box in the front of the room, or in a hole in the ground. He began to think Mr. Death had followed him home from Vietnam. People he loved and cared about died here too.

He spent the next couple of days preparing for his move to Waukegan. He rented a small U-Haul truck and finished packing. His cousin came over to help him hook up his car to the truck so he could tow it.

He was standing in the yard when his maa and dad came for a visit. His mother hugged him and cried. After he shook hands with his dad, he went to Cloquet with his cousin.

He met the same highway patrol trooper in the parking lot of the bank. All he said to Luke was, "You know, she didn't suffer."

But Luke did.

PART TWO

CHAPTER ELEVEN

It's been exactly six months since Carrie died. Why did she have to die? he thought. He grieved privately. He told no one at the Waukegan Police Department about his recent loss. He felt like Mr. Death was following him.

Luke was a patrolman in the sixty-five man (and woman) police force. He was happy to learn there were five other Vietnam veterans on the night shift, and three of them were Marines. Luke met Griff—Ralph Griffith, who had served with Echo Company, Second Battalion, Ninth Marines. He said he was an 0331, a machine gunner. He proudly proclaimed he had carried an M60 for democracy. Ron Taylor was a wing wiper from the Third Marine Air Wing, and Zac Thompson was a grunt from the Kilo Company, Third Battalion, Third Marines. Finally, at least there were three men who had his back.

◇◇

Waukegan, Illinois, was just north of Chicago. At first, Luke was assigned to walk the downtown beat. He learned that was where new patrolmen were initially assigned.

He walked from 2230 until 0630 up and down Main Street. He was also responsible for the streets on each side of Main and the alleys in between. His beat was eight blocks long. It was mostly businesses but there was also a bus depot and a couple of bars. The Black Cat had mostly black customers and the Town Pump had white customers. His primary duty was to rattle the front and back doors of the businesses to make sure they were locked. He occasionally assisted the other officers when their patrol cars responded to calls in his beat area.

One night as he was walking along pulling on business doors, he noticed an unmarked patrol car pull into the alley. He slid behind the building and waited for it to pull up to him. He liked being out of sight. When the car stopped Luke saw it was two detectives who were on the night shift: Miller and Mason.

He walked over, recognized one of them, and greeted Detective Mason.

"Hello, Detective Mason—all secure on my beat."

"We wanted to warn you about something on this beat," replied the detective. "It's happened a couple of times over the years. The burglars' MO is to grab the beat policeman, handcuff him with his own cuffs, and shoot him with his own gun so they can hit one of these jewelry stores."

"The last two times the bad guys jumped on the train in Chicago, pulled their job, and caught the train back to Chicago before someone found the beat policeman," added the other detective. He was called Shorty because he was tall—six two, six three.

"No shit," said Luke. His apprehension meter clicked up a couple of notches when he heard this. He felt a squirt of adrenaline enter his bloodstream.

"Just be careful—be especially careful coming around the corner of a building, that's how they got the last guy," added Mason.

"No shit," said Luke again.

As he walked along he expected someone to grab him at each place a bad guy might hide. He was ready.

A couple nights later when nothing happened, he began to relax—but not totally. He was always prepared for something to happen.

Luke had found an apartment just a few blocks from the police station so he was once again able to walk to work. It was a small place but Luke didn't need a large place to wrestle his memories of the 'Nam.

One night Luke was walking his beat, remembering what Detective Mason was telling him about how the last beat police-man died. He was always prepared when he came to the corner of a building. He usually took the corners wide, stepping three feet away from the building; other times he would sneak up on the corner, stepping around suddenly.

At one alleyway he got a surprise. A man was standing there. He had one arm above his head. Luke didn't hesitate. He charged right in. He hit the man's torso with his shoulder, knocking him down. He cuffed him with his hands behind his back. He rolled him over after searching for weapons.

It was a white male—late fifties, early sixties. His grungy appearance told Luke he was one of the harmless drunks that hung around downtown. Patrolman Warmwater felt bad, taking out an old drunk like that. He helped him to his feet.

"What the hell you doing? I was just taking a piss," said the old drunk.

"Public urination is against the law," advised Luke.

Luke called for a squad car to transport the now-identified Martin Mickleson to jail.

He felt bad about that arrest. Martin was sentenced to thirty days in jail. But he thanked Luke for arresting him. "Now I can get some good food and sleep in a real bed for a while," Martin said.

During the months after when Luke would see Martin on the street, he would slip him a five-dollar bill and say, "Happy birthday," or, "Some people found this in the park, they said it belonged to you. So, I'm just returning your property." Both smiled.

Because of the federal government's Relocation Program Luke had two sisters living in Chicago. On his two days off each week, Luke would drive down to visit. He needed to stay in touch with family since he was so far from home. Doris lived on the North Side of Chicago near Broadway and Lawrence Avenue. There were a lot of other Indian families in the area. Luke's other sister lived on the South Side near Gary, Indiana. So, one week he would visit one sister and the next week he would visit the other.

Sometimes they would go to a bar to drink and shoot pool. Luke usually won the pool games because he wasn't drinking. Sometimes they'd go to a bowling alley to relax and knock over some pins.

It was his way of keeping his sanity in the crazy world of Waukegan law enforcement.

Finally, Luke was assigned to a squad car on the night shift. A new recruit was now rattling the doors downtown.

Luke and his new partner, Dale Sheehan, checked out the car. The way it worked was, one drove and the other wrote the reports. Sheehan had joined the police department two weeks before Luke arrived. He was senior to Luke and reminded him of it as soon as they got together.

"I've been a Waukegan patrolman longer than you so I'm senior to you," Dale Sheehan said.

"That may be true, but I was on the road for three years before I came to Waukegan."

Luke looked at the other patrolman and decided some people just can't wear a uniform. Sheehan's pants had no creases; his shirt and tie looked like they'd been with him when he was eating spaghetti.

Luke asked, "What did you shine your shoes with? A turd?"

Sheehan raised one shoe and rubbed the toe on the back of his pants to knock the dust off. He did the same to other shoe.

Since he was on a roll, Luke continued, "Why didn't you get a hat that fits? That one's too big."

"No, it isn't—just have to put this toilet paper in the leather headband," simpered Sheehan.

"When was the last time you cleaned your pistol? Have you ever fired it? Anyone ever show you how to clean it?" asked Luke.

Dale Sheehan puffed out his chest and said, "I came in fourth in recruit school marksmanship competition," he bragged.

"Yeah, I heard there were just six in your class in recruit school."

"Well, how about you? When was the last time you cleaned your pistol?"

"Last night, both of them." Luke lifted his right pant leg to show Sheehan the snub-nosed .38 pistol in a brown ankle holster.

"Wow, I didn't know you carried a second gun."

"Better to have it and not need it than to need it and not have it," answered Luke. Just like the 'Nam, thought Luke, better to carry four grenades rather than just two.

Both patrolmen checked the black-and-white patrol car; the lights all worked. Luke hit the siren for a brief squeal. They checked the air pressure in the tires, made sure the spare had air.

"I'm driving because I'm senior to you—you write the reports tonight," said Sheehan.

"That's not the way it works; we take turns driving," answered Luke.

"But I'm senior to you and I decided I would drive."

"It doesn't matter, I'm going to drive," replied Luke. "Shall we go inside and ask the desk sergeant to settle this dispute?"

"No, go ahead and drive. But remember, I'm senior to you."

"You will never be senior to me, ever," Luke said, slamming the car door as an exclamation point.

Luke drove to their assigned area. He had his eyes scanning in every direction. If he were still in the Marine Corps, he would have called it "going tactical."

As he drove along he thought about his companion, his fellow Waukegan policeman, this Dale Sheehan guy. Luke didn't trust him. He couldn't count on him if the feces hit the electric spinning machine. Luke thought he would like a new partner—one of the other Vietnam veterans, preferably.

They were approaching Lewis Avenue when they saw a dark car approaching fast from the left. The driver didn't see them or he would have slowed down.

Luke turned onto Lewis Avenue and began pursuing the vehicle. He was about three blocks behind the speeding car. Luke remembered the code word for describing a vehicle: CYMBAL. The car was green, looked to be about five years old, a Chevy, a four-door, and he couldn't see the license plate yet.

He caught up to the car and turned on his red lights, lit up the back window with his spotlight. Luke had a good clock on him, he was doing forty-five miles an hour in a thirty zone.

As soon as the red lights came on, the Chevy's right turn signal blinked on. Once the car was stopped Luke pulled in behind him, careful to leave his car parked a little to the left, creating a safety zone so he could approach the car without standing out in the traffic lane.

Luke got out and walked up to the car. He carried his flashlight and stood by the driver's window; he was slightly behind the window so the driver had to turn and look out at him. Luke could see the driver was alone in the car, had both hands on the steering wheel. Luke got close enough so he could smell for alcohol. He took a deep sniff—nope, no beer or booze or weed smell.

"Good evening, sir, the reason I stopped you was you were doing forty-five miles an hour in a thirty zone."

"Yeah, I guess you're right, I wasn't paying attention."

"May I see your license and registration please?

The driver took out his wallet and handed Luke his license, dug behind the sun visor and gave Luke the registration card. Luke noticed the driver's license had a twenty-dollar bill paper-clipped to it.

Luke took the twenty and dropped it in the driver's lap, said, "I don't want your money."

Luke heard the patrol-car door open on the passenger side. Good, he thought, my partner's covering me. He walked back to his car and was surprised to see Officer Sheehan getting into the driver's seat. Luke stopped, turned, and walked back to the speeder's car. He gave the driver back his license and said, "I'm going to give you a break. Slow down and be careful."

"Thank you, Officer."

As the car signaled for a return to the traffic lane Luke walked back to driver's window of the patrol car. He told Sheehan he was the driver and asked him to get out. He had his hands on the windowsill of the patrol car. Using his flashlight, Sheehan rapped Luke's fingers. When Luke felt the pain, he pulled his hand away, punched Sheehan in the ear, and grabbed him by the shirt and hair, pulled him out of the car through the window. He stepped back and let Sheehan fall to the street.

"I'm the driver," Luke told Sheehan.

Sheehan got up and walked around the car and got back into the passenger's seat. Luke got into the patrol car and drove toward the police station. He looked at Sheehan and said, "This isn't working, I can't work with you. Let's see if the desk sergeant will change our assignments."

Luke was assigned to work with Donovan "Sneakers" Lloyd, a patrolman with five years on the force. He believed in doing the bare minimum when it came to police work: he would write just enough parking tickets, just enough moving violations to get by. His main effort in thwarting crime was to sneak up on people making love in cars. He had a regular circuit of places to check for steamed-up windows. Since Donovan did only enough, they made no felony arrests, didn't take any guns off the street.

"Is this why you became a policeman?" asked Luke.

"Yeah, it's so much fun to catch them lovers, it's thrilling to watch them scramble to get their clothes back on. Sometimes you even get a glimpse of the Promised Land."

Luke thought there was something wrong with Donovan. Catching lovers was not why Luke joined the police department. He discreetly asked the desk sergeant for another assignment. There were no open spots on the roster so Luke rode as roving patrol; he went anywhere in the city and normally backed up the other patrolmen. His car number was 411, and he was assigned to ride alone. He liked that.

He went back to making felony arrests. One month he won Patrolman of the Month for taking the most guns off the street. Another month he won the award for catching the most burglars.

One busy night Luke got a call on the radio. "Four-one-one, return to the station and see the desk sergeant."

"Four-one-one, ten-four."

Luke came in and met the desk sergeant. He asked Luke, "Do you know how to use this?" He reached under the counter to show Luke a Thompson submachine gun and two extra magazines.

"Yeah, the Marine Corps still had some in their inventory, we trained with them. They fire from an open-bolt position, forty-five caliber, and climb when fired."

"Good. Take this and go to Third and State—the firemen reported someone with long guns coming out of a fourth-floor apartment. They're afraid of getting shot at while fighting the trash fire in the alley behind the bank building. Go on down there and protect the firemen, and be careful with that thing," he said, pointing at the submachine gun.

Luke drove to the scene. He was thinking that the city was really serious about fighting crime to have a weapon like this. He got out of the patrol car and walked to the fire truck and reported to the assistant chief.

"Where did you see the people with long guns?

"Up in that apartment building next to the bank. They were coming down the fire escape. Haven't seen them lately but you never know."

"Okay, got you covered."

Luke walked over to a dark part of the alley, stood behind a telephone pole, and positioned himself where he could still see everything. His heart was thumping in his chest with the thought that he might actually have to use that weapon. He breathed deeply.

The firefighters put out the fire and began rolling up their hoses. As they were boarding their trucks, the assistant chief came up to thank Luke for covering their backs.

"No sweat, all in a night's work," Luke told the chief. He took the Thompson back to the desk sergeant.

"I knew you were in the Marine Corps and could handle that weapon." the sergeant said.

Luke smiled and went out to his patrol car. He drove around waiting for the bump he got from adrenaline to go away.

"Four-one-one, a call came in reporting a purse snatching in the parking lot of the hospital. The detectives are there now talking to the victim."

"Four-one-one, ten-four, got a description of the suspect?"

"Four-one-one, the suspect is described as a black male, about five foot nine. One hundred eighty pounds, black hair, brown eyes."

"Four-one-one, got a clothing description?"

"Four-one-one, ten-four, the suspect has been described as being naked."

"Four-one-one, naked? As in barefooted all over?"

"Four-one-one, ten-four, that is correct, no clothing"

"Four-one-one, ten-four."

Luke drove to the hospital; the parking lot surrounded the five-story building. He drove slowly through the rows of cars but didn't see anything suspicious. He parked his car, took out his flashlight, and began searching the alleys leading away from the hospital. As he was walking through the third alley he noticed a brown foot sticking out from behind a dumpster. He drew his pistol and got closer. He saw a black male lying behind the garbage container. He turned the corner and saw the man was using a purse to cover his genitals.

"Okay, asshole, drop the purse and get up against the wall—that's it, lean into the wall, spread your arms and legs. I don't have to search you, I can see you're unarmed. I won't ask you for an ID either—you don't have any pockets."

Luke handcuffed the suspect and led him back to his squad car. There was a heavy smell of fear coming from the man. He put him in the backseat and went back and picked up the purse.

The suspect in the backseat began talking fast to Luke, "Let me tell you what happened."

Luke had never arrested a naked man but he pretended like it happened all the time.

"Four-one-one, I have a suspect in custody on the north side of the hospital."

"Four-one-one, ten-four, stand by there, the detectives will be bringing the victim to identify the purse and suspect."

After Luke hung up the microphone, he said, "Go ahead, tell me what happened. Remember, you have the right to remain silent as long as you can stand the pain."

"See, I was in the next block there. I was visiting this woman, we had a few drinks and pretty soon we were in bed. Then we heard the front door opening, her husband was home early from work. I pushed my clothes under the bed and went out and hid on the fire escape. I heard him walking towards the window. I went down the steps. My weight lowered the damn thing. I heard the window open so I stepped off the fire escape. As soon as my weight came off, the damn thing went back up in the air. So there I was standing naked in the alley wondering what to do. Then this other naked guy came running by, saw me, and then handed me the purse. I ran down the alley and hid behind the Dumpster where you found me. I never saw that guy before or again."

The detectives came driving up, a woman got out of the backseat and walked over to Luke's patrol car. She looked in and said, "That's my purse and that's the bastard that stole it."

Luke went to the trunk of his car and covered the naked man up with a blanket and drove him to jail.

CHAPTER TWELVE

In time, Luke Warmwater and Ralph Griffith became partners. They rode together most nights and had the same days off. Both were Marines and had spent thirteen months in Vietnam in a grunt company.

Ralph said he carried an M60 machine gun and much ammo. He was in Bravo Company, First Battalion, First Marines. In the many nights they spent in the patrol car, they talked about their experiences over and over again. Both had been affected by their time in the war.

"We used to do these hunter-killer teams south of Da Nang," said Griff.

"What did you do?" asked Luke, always ready for a good war story so he could tell one of his own.

"Two of us would go crawling out of perimeter toward the VC village because we knew it was Vietcong infested.

"Yeah, what did you carry?"

"We both had a forty-five, two frags, one Willy Peter grenade, and a Ka-Bar."

"How did it feel without your weapon?"

"Naked, I felt naked without that machine gun. I went to see my buddy who worked at the armory, so I arrived in-country with selector switches for everyone—we all had automatic M14 rifles in my squad."

"So, how did you work those hunter-killer things?" asked Luke.

"We'd go crawling out on a dark night, find our way through our wire and mines. We'd take a long time to crawl towards the VC village. Just two crazy grunt Marines looking for someone to kill. As we got close to the village we would just lay and listen. Pretty soon we could hear the sound of someone sleeping. The snores, breathing noises, the night noises, even an occasional fart."

"That must have been some hairy shit knowing you were out there alone," Luke said.

"It felt like we were doing what young Marines were supposed to be doing. From the noise we could tell which end was the head and which was the feet. The way I did it was to put one hand over the mouth so they wouldn't make a noise, with the other hand I would stick them in the neck with my Ka-Bar. Usually there would be a spray of blood as I sliced through the arteries. It didn't take long for them to bleed out. My partner would be just outside the hooch covering my back. Then it would be his turn in the next hooch. Sometimes we would go in together because there was more than one guy sleeping in there. When we could we would leave one VC still asleep. Can you imagine how he felt when he woke up with his friends dead around him?

"Then we could crawl back to our wire. I could smell the VC blood on me. I was full of blood on the outside and adrenaline on the inside."

Luke was the quiet one of the two. Ralph was loud, brash, and was exceedingly polite—overly polite.

◇◇

During one of the evening briefings before they hit the streets, the desk sergeant said he got a directive from the mayor.

He told Luke and Ralph to be especially watchful in their patrol area because, according to the mayor, transvestites were targeting the sailors from Great Lakes Naval Base as the swabbies passed through Waukegan. The transvestites would solicit the sailors, take them back to an apartment, and jackroll them.

The desk sergeant was explicit: "If you see any of these men dressed as women, bring them in, Charge them with anything you want just so we get them off the streets."

Luke and Griff checked the patrol car. They had the area that included downtown and Sheridan Road where the transvestites lured sailors.

Sure enough, they saw a sailor wearing his white uniform on the corner. One he/she had his hand down the sailor's pants. The sailor was kissing the other one.

"What a lucky sailor, I can't attract two women," said Griff.

"Those two men are women only in that sailor's mind."

"Okay, you heard the mayor … arrest them!"

Griff and Luke approached the threesome.

"Hey, swabbie, still got your wallet?"

"Yes, I do."

"Quit kissing that man and catch a cab back to base."

The swabbie patted his wallet in his front pocket, thanked the policemen, and went to the corner to flag down a cab.

Luke informed the two that they were under arrest. They searched them and handcuffed them. Griff decided to search one a little more.

"Sir, would you remove your bra please?"

The man unhooked his bra, slipped the straps down his arm. When he was handing it to Griff something fell out of the cups. It was a plastic vial that contained a white powder; the other cup held a baggie of marijuana.

Possession of a controlled substance was added to the charges of disorderly conduct and lewd and lascivious behavior.

After the two men were booked, Luke and Griff went outside back to their car.

"Sir, would you remove your bra, please?" said Luke.

"How else would you say it?"

"You were remarkably polite to that man. I never thought I'd hear such a thing."

Luke had a court appearance but was released early from his obligation when the suspect decided to plead guilty. He had the afternoon free and didn't want to go back to his empty apartment. He didn't have enough time to go see his sisters in Chicago. He hadn't been on the police force long enough to make any real friends except Griff.

He decided to stop for coffee and found a café nearby. He walked in, looked around, and selected a table where he could see most of the room and the front entrance. Good fields of fire, Luke thought. He could see anyone approaching his position.

There weren't many people in the place, but one couple attracted his attention. The man was older than the woman and they seemed to be having a business meeting. The man was dressed in a gray lawyer's suit. He kept looking at his watch, obviously letting everyone know he was a busy man. This was confirmed when the man put some papers in a briefcase, zipped it shut, and stood up. He reached across and shook hands with the woman. She was talking to his back as he was walking away.

The woman smiled and Luke looked closer. The most obvious part of her was her hair: it was flaming red. It looked thick, shiny-bright, coppery, and healthy. She was attractive in a unique kind of way. Her skin was pale as a piece of paper and her eyes were blue and heavily made up, thick lashes and black mascara. She had traces of freckles on her cheeks. She was wearing a gold anklet around one ankle and had many jangly, noisy bracelets. She moved her hands, arms, and shoulders when she talked. She was wearing a light blue suit with a white blouse. She had dangly earrings and a string of pearls around her neck. When she had stood up to shake the man's hand Luke noticed she was tall, five nine, maybe five ten—almost as tall as him. She wasn't fat or skinny, just curvy.

Luke was intrigued by her magnetic appearance. He wanted to talk to her, to get to know her better. Her eyes said what he was thinking. She gracefully indicated a chair at her table. He picked up his water glass and walked on over.

Luke sat down without saying a word. She began talking immediately.

"Hi, I'm Abbey Donna Gidoon. I don't like my first name, sounds too churchy, so you can call me Donna. What's your name, and, if I may be so bold, are you an American Indian?

"Luke Warmwater, and yup," he answered.

"The reason I asked is when I was a little girl my parents had a cabin up north near the Red Cliff Reservation in Wisconsin. All summer long we enjoyed the Northwoods. I got to make friends with some Ojibwe girls too. Where are you from?"

"I'm from the Fond du Lac Reservation in Minnesota, about ninety miles west of Red Cliff."

"What are you doing here so far from home? I'm from Indianapolis, but now I feel like this is my home. My parents still live down there. I have one sister who lives in Chicago."

"I came to Great Lakes Naval Hospital to visit a Marine I knew who was wounded in Vietnam. I liked the city so much I decided to stay."

"How long were you in Vietnam?" she asked.

"Too long."

"Well, what kind of job did you find?

"I'm a police officer for the City of Waukegan."

"Uh-oh," she said. "I'm a paralegal at the public defender's office. I guess we should be sworn enemies because we work on opposite sides of the law. Is it true opposites attract? I wanted to meet and talk with you as soon as I saw you come in. Did you know you move like a slinky panther or some other big cat? But I don't know about your job—you arrest them and we defend them. I really like my job there, we mostly lose in court but once in a while the attorneys pull off a win."

She continued, "Did you see the man that just left? He's my attorney."

"A paralegal needing an attorney? Now that sounds serious," Luke said.

"He's handling my divorce. My husband left me after three months. Later I found out he was leaving me for another man, which was a huge surprise to me. The marriage lasted three months and was never consummated."

"You mean you never …"

"Not even once," she said.

"But you're so young and beautiful."

"Thank you for your kind words. On a good day I know I can look pretty good—almost pretty.

"My husband married me to hide his attraction to men. He sounds happy, he said he and his lover are moving to San Francisco. We're selling our house and splitting the profits. This is going to be a quiet divorce, no screaming or fighting about things. How about you?"

"I'm single. I was engaged to a wonderful woman, we were going to get married in December."

"What happened?"

"She was killed in a car accident back home. I came to Waukegan to get away from the memories. I feel like Mr. Death has been following me around ever since the war."

"I think you chose the wrong profession—I'm sure you see your share of car crashes, gunfights, and robberies."

Both were surprised they were talking about their lives on such a deep level so quickly. They each wondered about it then just decided to go with the flow.

"What shift do you work? What are your days off? I'd like to spend some time with you," said Donna.

"My days off are Wednesday and Thursday this month, then Friday and Saturday next month. It changes every month and I don't know why. So, what are you interested in? We could explore Chicago or Milwaukee—there are plenty of state parks around too," Luke suggested.

She took out a business card, flipped it over, and wrote her home phone number down. Luke wrote his home number on the front of his business card because the back of the card had a printed Miranda warning on it.

She looked at it and began to read it out loud, "You have the right to remain silent."

Luke laughed and said, "I'm being silent."

She raised one eyebrow and looked at Luke suspiciously. "You're not one of those mean kind of cops, are you? Do you thump people?"

"No, I don't let myself or my partner get hurt, but I don't go out of my way to hurt other people."

"I felt that about you. Would you like another cup of coffee?" she asked.

"No, I had enough—enough so that my eyes are brown."

She looked at his eyes and laughed at his corny joke. She drained the last of her coffee, stood up, gathered her things, and looked at Luke. He picked up his bill for coffee and walked her to the cash register. She took out her wallet and paid for her coffee; Luke paid for his. They walked together toward her car, a VW Bug.

"When will you call me so we can do something together?" she asked.

"How about right now?"

"I wouldn't hear it ring," she smiled.

Luke picked up an imaginary phone and dialed the number while looking at her card. "Riiinnng!" he said.

She picked up her imaginary phone. "Hello?"

"Hello, Donna. This is Luke Warmwater. Want to go to lunch?"

"Let me check my schedule—wait, this is my day off. Where would you like to go for lunch then? I know a couple of good places downtown. You're not vegetarian are you? My ex-husband was and we could never go out to eat. I like prime rib and any cut of steak. Listen to me go on and on—didn't even give you a chance to answer. Bill's Steak House is excellent. Where are you parked? I see a car with Minnesota license plates, is that your car?"

"Yes, I'll follow you," he said.

They had a good meal together and decided to spend the rest of the afternoon and evening together until he had to go home and put on his uniform. Luke never knew a woman who could talk so much; he liked it since he didn't have to talk at all. He began his tour, an eight-hour shift.

"I just drop it in their lap and tell them I don't want their money," replied Luke.

"Most of the guys in this police department take the money,"

"Really? What do you do with it?"

"I'm like you: drop it into their laps then write the ticket."

"I've noticed something else. Me and one guy I was riding with—it was Stewart—were chasing a burglar. We got to the place and used the broken back door to go inside. Stewart stopped to go through the desks. He was looking for rolls of stamps or the petty cash box."

"Catch the burglar?"

"Nah, he got away. If the guy was watching the door we would have caught him. But no, he was too busy looking for something to steal. I don't like riding with those kinds of guys."

"Get used to it, the whole department is like that."

"Really?" Luke was surprised.

"Yeah, most of them think that's one of the side benefits of the job. It isn't just the cops, either. The lawyers, the state attorneys, most judges—the whole system is fucked. Everyone is fucked."

"Not me, I don't play that way. My maa raised me right."

"Me neither, I like to think I'm honest," agreed Griff.

The two continued checking the back doors and windows business district. The radio was quiet.

"In-country, we had C-ration cans dating back to the Korean but most were from the mid-fifties," said Luke.

"guess they were better than eating the gooker food, or said Griff.

"st guys didn't eat those Ham and Lima Bean meals. I myself to like them—I always had plenty of food to eat. trade my peaches and get four cans of those Ham and beans."

"in a while we had to drink rice-paddy water. It was choppers couldn't get in because of the weather."

CHAPTER THIRTEEN

The Waukegan black-and-white police car was idling through an alley. Both occupants had their spotlights trained on the back doors and windows of the businesses on the block. It v just another midweek patrol for the pair in the center sect the city.

It was about an hour into the shift. Luke and Griff comfortable working with each other: they'd been thro enough to trust each other, to know what the other c

The day's temperature had peaked in the low ni

"Ever notice the people on the street get goofy hot?" Griff asked.

"Yeah, I noticed that. Full moons have that

They passed the time in conversation, both listening to the sounds of radio calls. None of them so they just patrolled.

"Are you getting used to the rat race h asked Griff.

"Yeah, everyone always looks like th thing," answered Luke.

"You'll get used to it. Pretty soon for somewhere."

"I can hardly wait. You know v

"What's that, Marine?"

"How many people have m licenses, as if they expect me to stopped them."

"What do you do with i

"I used to wish for a tall glass of water, ice cubes floating. I wished it so many times I bet I could draw a picture of one today."

"Six-oh-three." The dash-mounted radio called out their patrol car number.

"Six-oh-three, Fourteenth and Adams," answered Griff, giving their location.

"Six-oh-three, go to the Projects, apartment three-oh-six, domestic disturbance, neighbors called."

"Six-zero-three, ten-four, on the way."

Griff said, "Domestic, eh? I'd rather go to an armed robbery any old day."

"Yeah, each one is different," answered Luke.

Luke drove to the Projects, a public housing area. Most of the people in the apartments were poor—had to be to live there.

"I wonder how this will end up with the negroes? Oops, are they now black people, or Afro Americans?" asked Griff.

"Yeah, calling people what they call themselves always works for me," answered Luke.

Luke was weaving the patrol car through traffic; he had his red lights on but not the siren. Using the siren in the city was iffy because people got surprised and did crazy things, like hitting the brakes, turning in front of the patrol car—hard to tell what they were going to do.

It took a little over three minutes to get to the location.

"Six-zero-three. Out of the car at the Projects, apartment three-zero-six."

"Six-oh-three, your backup is tied up with a motor vehicle accident at Ninth and Wilson."

"Six-zero-three, ten-four."

Both patrolmen grabbed their nightsticks and flashlights when they got out of the car. They ran up the three flights of stairs to get to the apartment, with Luke in the lead. Griff was looking around as they climbed and saw people peeking out of their windows and doors.

Luke and Griff could hear loud, angry-sounding voices coming from above them as they continued to climb.

"I'll take him, you take her," Luke told Griff. "We'll trade next time."

Luke pounded on the door with his nightstick. He did it again when no one answered.

The woman pulled the door open and Luke moved toward her. She was about five feet six, maybe two hundred pounds, wearing a yellow dress that had one sleeve ripped off. She looked agitated.

In a loud, rapid talking voice, she said, "'Rest that mother fucka—he hit me and ripped my dress."

"Where is he?" asked Luke, while rapidly scanning the room. Griff came up behind him and led the woman to the kitchen.

"Please, ma'am, can we go in the kitchen? I need to take your statement."

The man coming out of the bedroom was huge: about six three, 240 pounds. He was wearing a white sleeveless T-shirt that showed monster arms and slabs of muscle. He was shiny with sweat. He was wearing blue jeans and black work boots. Luke thought this was going to be an ugly situation.

The man looked angry; his face looked mean. He was scowling.

"Ain't no motherfucker gonna take me to jail, I don't need that kind of shit," he said in a deep voice.

"If you come along quietly there won't be any more trouble."

"Fuck you," said the large man, taking a swing at Luke.

He caught the man's hand and pulled; he was using the man's momentum to bring him down to the floor. When the man hit the floor, Luke jumped on him, landing with his knees in the middle of the larger man's back and knocking the wind out of him. Luke grabbed one arm and pulled it back and placed a handcuff on his wrist. He grabbed the other arm but the man resisted until Griff came running in and also landed on the man's back. The impact knocked the wind out of him again, and it was a simple twist to lock the second handcuff on the man.

Luke heard noises from the kitchen. He looked up to see the woman coming at them, a butcher knife in her hand, her arm raised like she was going to stab someone with that knife. Her eyes were wide open. She half screamed at the two police officers, "Leave my man alone!" while waving the butcher knife in jagged circles.

Both Luke and Griff scrambled on the other side of the handcuffed suspect. They had their pistols drawn and were yelling at the woman.

"Drop the knife, please drop the knife!" shouted Griff.

"One more step towards us and I'm shooting her," Luke told Griff.

She stopped and saw two policemen kneeling on the floor with two big pistols, both had the hammers cocked back on their .357s, and they were pointing them at her. Her eyes opened wider; she didn't know what to do. She was mad but didn't want to get shot.

"Fuck you motherfuckers," she said, as she threw the knife into the kitchen.

Griff jumped up, grabbed an arm and pulled it behind her, grabbed the other one and cuffed that one also. Griff later said he could smell the fear in her sweat, it was quite pungent.

Luke helped the man to his feet; Griff asked for the house keys so they could lock the place up. The woman pointed to a series of nails, and Griff picked off the one she indicated was the house key.

They walked out of the apartment, Griff stopping to lock the door. Luke noticed people coming out of their apartment to watch the activity. The crowd began gathering on the porches and stairs of the Projects. It quickly grew to forty or fifty people.

They were yelling at the two police officers; the words "fucking pigs" were heard frequently.

"I don't like the looks of this, Griff," said Luke.

"Let's get down to the squad car; I feel so lonely without my shotgun," Griff answered. "Watch it—someone's throwing bottles at us."

"Yeah, rocks too," Luke said, while ducking his head to avoid the incoming rock.

The sound of broken bottles crashed and echoed through the hot, dark night. The windshield of the patrol car had jagged cracks where a full bottle of beer connected. Luke got the two suspects in the car's backseat. They were ducking from the rocks and bottles hitting the car.

Luke reached in and took out the 12 gauge shotgun. He fired one round in the air. Griff was on the radio calling for assistance.

It was a standoff. The patrolmen couldn't leave with their prisoners, and the people didn't get any closer because of the loud shotgun. Luke simply aimed the shotgun at the people who were throwing things at them. He didn't shoot, but by aiming at them, he made them scatter.

Luke could hear sirens approaching from three directions. Griff muttered, "I hope the Dog Man is on duty tonight."

"I think he is, I saw him checking his patrol car out as we were leaving the station this evening."

The Dog Man, Earl Willow, arrived with a squeal of tires sliding on the hot blacktop. Both Luke and Griff could hear the huge German shepherd named Killer barking in the backseat. Earl got out, opened the door for the snarling dog. He snapped a fifty-foot leash on the excited canine. Earl loosened the leash and Killer began running toward people, barking and snapping his teeth. The crowd melted back into the adjoining streets and their apartments. The bottles and rocks quit bouncing around the patrol car.

Luke was able to drive his car up and over the curb, turn onto the sidewalk, and drive to the alley. There were at least five police cars parked around the Projects with their red lights flashing.

Somebody's going to jail, Luke thought. A lot of somebodies by the looks of it.

"Glad we got out of there with no one getting hurt," Luke said.

"Me too—glad it wasn't us anyway," answered Griff.

"Was it my shotgun or that mean old dog, Killer?

"Both."

After booking and jailing their prisoners they were someone else's worry. Luke and Griff got back in their car and continued patrolling.

The streets got quieter as the night grew later. Luke noticed a car weaving in front of them. "Once more across the centerline and I'm going to talk to that driver," Luke said.

Sure enough, the car drifted across the centerline. Luke turned in behind it and flipped on his red lights. Both cops turned on their spotlights and lit up the car. The car wasn't stopping, so Luke sounded the siren for a couple of seconds. The car began to pull over to the curb and Luke parked behind it. Positioning his car so he had a safety zone, he walked up and stopped so the driver had to look over his left shoulder at him. Luke didn't have to get any closer—he could smell beer coming from inside the car. Luke shined his flashlight in the backseat and could see full and empty cans.

The driver was alone in the car. Luke asked for his license and registration.

The driver took his license out of his wallet. Luke could see money paper-clipped to the license. One of those, he thought, another guy who thinks he can evade the law by handing over his license with money. Luke would never play that way. He took the fifty-dollar bill off the license and handed it to the man.

"Put that in your pocket, I don't want your money," Luke said in a disgusted voice, his lip curled in a sneer. He turned and walked back to run a check on the license plates. He noted that his partner was standing by the rear door of the car.

Griff had his back, Luke knew.

"Sir, would you get out of the car and put your hands on the trunk?"

The driver got out and walked unsteadily back to the rear of his car. Luke was walking behind the driver, because if the driver wanted to resist he would have to turn toward Luke. The driver didn't resist and once he had his hands on the car, Griff stepped forward and searched the man. He pulled his hands behind him and handcuffed the driver.

Luke got in the car and grabbed the radio microphone. "Six-zero-three, dispatch, I need a hook for a drunk driver's car in the nine hundred block of Sheridan Road.

"Dispatch, six-oh-three, ten-four, rolling a hook toward you."

"I only had a couple of beers but that car is drunk," the driver tried to explain to the two patrolmen while pointing at his car.

Both Griff and Luke laughed at the drunk driver's attempt at humor. They took him to jail where he was searched again and photographed; Griff got his cuffs back. Luke and Griff walked out to their car to resume their patrol.

"What're you going to do about working here?" asked Griff as they got back in the car.

"I think I'll quit before I start taking money or looking for rolls of stamps at a burglary scene," answered Luke. "My honesty is worth more than the damn money."

"I'm thinking of going up north to Wisconsin, some town must be looking for an experienced police officer," said Griff.

"I heard there are a couple of security officer jobs open at that new community college. I think I'll look into that job," said Luke.

Both were pissed because people wearing uniforms and badges just like them were only interested in stealing.

"Yeah, there's law and order and just us," Griff observed.

CHAPTER FOURTEEN

A few days later, Luke and Griff were on patrol in their assigned area in the middle third of Waukegan. They had just finished investigating a traffic accident.

"I like these kinds of accidents," said Luke.

"What? You like car accidents?" Griff asked.

"Yeah, low speed, didn't have to dig anyone out of a crumpled-up car. The kind where you don't need the meat wagon, just the hook to drag the dead car away."

"Like in the 'Nam when we had a long firefight with the VC and didn't need a medevac?"

"Exactly. No blood, no guts hanging around."

"I had a screamer of a nightmare last night."

"Did you actually scream, wake the neighbors?"

"No, just woke up with my heart pounding so hard it gave me a headache."

"Details?"

"Nah, it was enough to know that I was out of ammo, water, and friends."

"I had a few of those kind lately—only thing added was my Ka-Bar was dull too."

Griff was writing the accident report while Luke drove behind the shopping center near Lewis Avenue. He had set his spotlight so it aimed at the back doors and windows of the businesses. He could see the doors, and the reflection of his spotlight told him the windows were intact. They were just idling along.

It was about two A.M. as they checked the backs of buildings for burglars.

"I think I got a new girlfriend," Luke confessed.

"My old lady hates it whenever I get a new girlfriend," Griff joked.

Just then Luke noticed a back door was open about an inch. "Check it out," he said.

"Yup, looks like someone has an overnight visitor."

"Six-zero-three, dispatch, we got an open door at the back of Montgomery Ward."

"Six-oh-three, ten-four, rolling back up to you."

While Luke was watching the door, it flew open. A human figure came running toward them, then veered off to one side. The man was young and black and carried a sack.

"I got him," Griff said as he opened the door and began running after the burglary suspect. The young man ran out of the parking lot and into a small swamp behind the shopping center. He was weaving between the small shrubs. He was running fast. He didn't seem to mind the ankle-deep water. He leaped over the smaller plants. Griff was right behind him.

Luke was on the radio letting everyone know what was happening. He climbed up on the hood of the car and was yelling directions to Griff.

"He's to your right—about fifty feet ahead. Now he's turning left."

The suspect broke free of the swamp and began running through the playground. He got to the school and Luke heard a car start up. He saw the headlights come around the corner of the building. Griff was near the middle of the field when the driver apparently saw him. Now it was the burglar chasing the cop. Griff did a dive and roll to avoid getting hit by the car. The car made a looping turn to come back after Griff.

"Shoot the motherfucker, Griff!" yelled Luke from his perch on top of the police car. Griff drew his pistol and cranked off three quick rounds, waiting to see which way the car was going to go. Luke had his pistol out and fired off four rounds at the car. He saw one car window break and heard his other rounds hit the car. Griff fired again, hit a headlight, and starred the windshield. The car turned away from Griff, The car-chasing-the-cop game was over.

The burglary suspect drove to the street. Luke was on the radio telling everyone it was a green Ford Fairlane heading south on Lewis Avenue. He drove to Lewis Avenue then stopped and backed up to get his partner. Griff came up to the police car and got in. He was using a speedloader to replace the rounds he fired.

"I know I hit his car with all six of my rounds," said Griff, breathing deeply.

"I hit the car with four of my rounds," answered Luke. "Let's join the chase—the Dog Man can secure the building."

Luke was about to pull out onto Lewis Avenue when he saw someone coming fast. He hit the brakes and watched the detectives in their unmarked car following the chase. They must have been doing at least sixty miles an hour on that residential four-lane street. Luke could see the red lights flashing as the chase continued on Lewis Avenue. In all, there were three police cars chasing the suspect's vehicle.

"Looks like he's slowing down to turn left on Taylor. Yup, now he's heading east on Taylor," the lead police officer said on the radio. "We're doing sixty-five."

Another voice came on the radio. "We're at Tenth and Taylor, just saw the green Ford go by. He's turning north on Sheridan Road now."

Luke and Griff were chasing the chase.

"The driver's easing over to the passenger's side, I think he's gonna jump," a voice on the radio said. "We just slowed down to thirty."

"There he goes—he dove out of the car."

Griff and Luke watched the suspect roll in the grass strip between the concrete curb and sidewalk. He rolled and skidded in the grass for about fifteen feet. When he stopped, he sat up, shook his head, and rolled to his feet. He turned and headed for the backyard of a house. The detectives were right behind him. They watched him scale the fence separating the yards, then went over the fence after him.

"Look at his car," Griff said.

Luke looked and saw that the driverless car was headed toward a Chevrolet dealer's showroom. The car bounced off a parked car and hit the plate glass window. The car stopped when it hit a new yellow Corvette.

Luke and Griff slowed to look inside the dealer's showroom.

"The Corvette stopped it," said Griff.

"Oh, but that pretty car," answered Luke.

"That front fender isn't so pretty anymore."

"I'm glad we don't have to write that property damage report."

"Yeah, I think the lead car has to do that part."

"And the detectives have to write the report about the foot chase."

"All we got is the initial report on how the chase started."

"I'll do that one, you were the guy doing the foot chase."

"Nah, since we both fired at the car, we both have to write reports."

"Yup, like shitting, the job isn't done until the paperwork is finished."

"Remember that C-ration toilet paper?" asked Griff.

"Yeah, I once used it to plug a hole where a guy was bleeding."

"Isn't if funny how easy it is to remember stuff from the 'Nam?"

"Not funny."

The detectives came on the radio and said the suspect got away from them in the foot chase. One added that when last seen, the suspect was headed westbound; they could hear the dogs barking in the distance as he made his escape.

It was just getting light a few hours later on that spring morning. They would be off shift in an hour or so; they had finished writing the reports.

Luke said, "Griff." He pointed to a young black male who was walking down the street.

"He looks too nonchalant," said Griff.

"And the mud on his legs looks like the mud on your legs," Luke added.

"Don't look at him."

Luke hit the red lights and siren and roared away from the man they were talking about. About four blocks down the street he turned off the lights and siren. He made a right turn and cut through the alley and let Griff out a half-block ahead of the man they wanted to talk to.

Luke went around the block and came up behind the man who was too nonchalant. Luke noticed the grass stains on the man's elbows, knees, and butt. He squealed to a stop and gave a short blast on the siren. The man turned, saw the cop. He started running. Luke gave another blast on the siren. The man was coming to the end of the brick wall. He turned to see how close the police car was. Griff stepped out with his thirty-six-inch riot baton ready. He used the baton to aim at the man's solar plexus. The suspect saw him. He tried to stop. He ran into the baton. He almost folded in half, his feet were off the ground and he landed on his butt. Griff flipped him over and clicked on both handcuffs in a matter of seconds.

Luke lit up his red lights again and got out to look at the guy. He was curled in a U-shape but had his head back trying to suck in air. Both Griff and Luke looked down at the man trying to breathe.

"Body count one, partner," Luke said.

"It took awhile, but we got him."

"The radio said the Dog Man got five more hiding in the store."

Jim Northrup   137

"It was our call so we get the credit for six burglars tonight. Body count six."

When the man was done trying to take great breaths they picked him up and took him to the police car. They searched him, putting everything in his pockets on the hood of the car. In his wallet they found a driver's license that matched the name on the license-plate registration of the car that went through the Chevy dealer's showroom window.

They took the now-identified burglar to the station and booked him.

It was a satisfying night for the two young patrolmen.

"I think I'll celebrate by taking my new girlfriend out for breakfast," said Luke.

"Take her to that place where you first met her."

"Great idea. How do you think of stuff like that?"

"I don't know, ask either of my two ex-wives."

After changing out of his uniform Luke called Donna to ask her for a breakfast date. Instead of going out to eat she offered to cook breakfast for them at her apartment. Luke thought that was a great idea since he would get to know her better. He was whistling and smiling as he drove to her place.

When he rang her buzzer she clicked the lock to let him in the building. He tapped on the door and she opened it wide for him to come in.

"I'm glad you called, I was just trying to get my courage up to invite you over here."

They hugged. He liked her smell. It was a close hug that lasted a long time.

"What have you been doing? Any exciting cases?"

"No, nothing real unusual," he answered.

"Well, at the public defender's office we have a huge back-log of cases where your department overcharged them. It's like a game of let's make a deal, isn't that so?"

"I know something—the more we talk about our jobs, the less chance we have of getting to know each other.

Donna was quiet as she digested his words. She got up and poured him a cup of coffee, sat down, and offered him a chair. She looked at his smiling face, smiled back, and said, "Tell me about your high school years."

"Not much to say about school. I went to school and graduated," he said.

She sat a plate in front of him. The smell of the fluffy omelet, the bacon, toast, and coffee reminded him how long it had been since he had eaten last. It was midnight the night before. It was even longer than that since he'd eaten a home-cooked meal.

They ate their meal together; it signaled a new level of trust between them.

"What do you have planned for the day? It's my day off."

"Nothing planned," he said.

"I like plants," she said.

"I noticed." He looked around the room and tried to identify all the plants he could see in the kitchen and into the living room.

"If you like we could go to the botanical gardens in Milwaukee. I always like going there, always something new to see. I must have been there five times since last year at this time. The smells and the colors mesmerize me. I hope you like experiencing plants.

"Yup, sure do."

"We can go in Betsy, my VW Bug. It's the sweetest ride, never breaks down, never causes me any trouble. My dad told me to change the oil frequently and the car will last a very long time. I take it to the garage and they keep the car running for me.

"Your dad knew what he was talking about."

Luke and Donna drove to the botanical gardens and had a great time walking among the plants, seeing and smelling the many smells of the dirt and flowers. He kept it to himself, but he didn't like being in the greenhouse that held plants from the tropics. They looked and smelled like the ones he had seen in Vietnam, a place he was still trying to forget.

The two drove back to Waukegan. He had to get some sleep, so they arranged an evening date to get to know each other.

Luke went to his apartment to sleep. He set his alarm for four hours but woke up agitated by his nightmare. It was about that fucking war again.

Luke was scared, his insides were shaking. He tried calming down by deep breathing. The words of his platoon sergeant echoed through his mind. Everyone is afraid—it is what you do in spite of the fear that counts.

Luke listened to the quiet of the rice paddy. They were lying alongside a well-used trail. A local farmer told them the Vietcong used this trail all the time. Luke and his twelve Marines waited in the inky dark. It was a typical L-shaped ambush. The bottom of the L was anchored by their machine gun: the M60's field of fire was down the middle of the trail. There was a stake driven in the ground so the machine gunner wouldn't be shooting where the rest of the squad was lying in wait. Two Marines were lying next to each other facing the trail. Between the two, they had decided who would fire at hip level and who would fire at boot level. The two Marines at the end of the trail faced the brush to protect their flank.

They waited.

The machine gunner saw something moving on the trail toward him. He waited, then saw three more human shapes behind the first one—they were getting closer to the muzzle of his M60. He pulled the trigger and held it down. The red tracers told him where his bullets were going and hitting. The Marines along the long end of the L-shaped ambush began shooting. The gunfire, explosions, screams, and laughter added to the noise of the night. After the initial burst of fire, it got quiet. The mud Marines were changing the magazines on their M14 rifles, reloading.

Gunfire erupted on the right flank of their formation. Then a lot more gunfire added to the noise. The crump, crump sound of the exploding grenades was mixed in. Luke flinched when these went off. Uh-oh, he thought. What did we step into? The sound of the enemy weapons made him think a Vietcong squad was attacking his right flank. He had to break off the ambush and get the hell out of there. He clicked a couple of Claymore mines to cover their escape.

He passed the word to break it off and meet at the rally point. Luke and his squad crashed through the brush as they climbed the little hill. On top Luke began to establish a perimeter. The Marines knew what to do: some began digging fighting holes, others were redistributing the ammo. The corpsman was working on the wounded. The radioman was talking to the platoon commander.

They waited.

Like the Marines, the Vietcong gathered their dead and wounded and moved back from the firefight.

About an hour later they heard noises in the tree line. The Marines called in artillery. The rounds crashed in and when the explosions died down, they took turns sleeping.

◇◇

Luke was eager to get back to work so he could tell Griff about the great time he had with this new woman who was going to be his girlfriend.

Luke and Griff checked the equipment, lights, radio, and siren on the patrol car they would use during that night's shift. It was Griff's turn to drive.

"She's really something. When I think of something to say, she's already saying it. I like how her mind works. We're on the same wavelength or something," said Luke.

"What does she look like?"

She's tall, has red hair, blue or green eyes depending on what she's wearing. I can look deep into her eyes for a long time. Her voice is musical and she has the slightest accent. She has curves all over the where. I noticed she's left-handed."

"What? No scars, marks, or tattoos or any other identifying features?" asked Griff, always on duty.

"You're grilling me like a witness," said Luke.

"Okay, one final question. Have you spent the night with her? We have the same nights off, you know."

"Yes, and more than one night."

"Good. You don't have to say more—let's go fight crime."

CHAPTER FIFTEEN

Their night was typical, calls on the radio directed them to the scenes of things gone wrong, a burglary, a bar fight, a car accident. They worked smoothly together as the busy night went on.

"Six-oh-three," the radio dispatcher said.

"Six-zero-three, we're at Third and Washington."

"Six-oh-three, go to the rear of the Sears store on Lewis Avenue, assist the firefighters."

"Six-oh-three, ten-four."

"Wonder what this is all about?" asked Luke.

"I'll let you know in about two minutes and thirty-four seconds," said Griff as he hit the red lights and siren. The sweeping beacon of the lights and the high-pitched sound of the siren helped dump a pound of adrenaline into Luke's bloodstream. Griff was cracking his gum faster than usual as he wheeled the patrol car through the streets. He turned down a narrow alley and told Luke, "This comes out in the middle of the back parking lot."

They arrived on the scene to see the firefighters spraying water on a smoldering Dumpster and the rear wall of the retail store. Firemen were on the roof chopping a vent hole; they also had a hose with them and began spraying down into the structure. The water seemed to have no effect on the fire. A fifteen-foot section of the wall collapsed. The fire was winning the battle.

The patrol sergeant called them over and told them, "Take the north end of the parking lot, keep everyone back. I'll take the south end until another patrol car arrives."

Griff drove to the north end of the building. They got out and stretched a clothesline to create a barrier as the first gawkers arrived to watch the firemen fight the blaze that was growing larger. They walked up and down the line, keeping the bystanders on the correct side of it. They could feel the heat from the fire.

Suddenly there was a crack of an explosion. Luke and Griff jumped and looked around for a hole to dive into. The firefighters on the roof had moved away from the hole they had chopped. The roof was sagging near where the wall had fallen down across the alley.

Griff and Luke were keeping the crowd away from the dangerous fire.

"Does this heat remind you of a napalm strike?" Griff asked Luke.

"Yup, especially one of those close ones," said Luke.

While pushing back a crowd that was attempting to move closer to the fire, the two police officers were approached by a man. He kept looking back at the store as he talked with them. He explained that he was the owner and was looking to hire them to protect his store when they got off work.

The two Marines agreed and were hired on the spot to guard the store. As the shift ended both officers parked their patrol car at the station and turned in their reports covering the previous night's action. They agreed to meet at the scene of the fire.

When Luke got to the store, Griff was already waiting. Luke handed him a couple of hamburgers, some fries, and coffee.

"When we get off here today I'll take you out to eat," he promised Luke.

After about an hour Luke saw a pickup truck creeping down the alley.

"Doesn't the shift sergeant have a truck like that?

"Yeah, that's him driving it."

"I wonder what he's doing?"

"Looks like he's going into the building. Let's talk to him."

"Good morning, Sergeant, can we help you?" asked Luke.

"No, just going in to do a little shoplifting—it's my wife's birthday and I haven't had time to get her anything," replied the sergeant.

"We were hired to protect the building," said Luke

"Good, keep everyone out until I get done," said the sergeant.

Griff elbowed Luke in the ribs and gave him the nod. Luke understood and both police officers left the sergeant to his shoplifting.

"Hey, Griff—I bet he didn't have permission to be in there shopping."

"Sometimes you have to overlook things to avoid future problems. He probably won't be the only one who comes shopping."

Griff's prediction proved accurate: at least five more cars and trucks pulled up behind the building. Even the shift captain arrived with his pickup truck. Six cops were in the building and began coming out with plundered merchandise.

The burglar-cops were laughing and teasing each other as they began loading the items into their private vehicles. One patrolman had a key-cutting machine. "I can duplicate any key you need," he bragged.

Griff told Luke, "We're just here to keep the civilians out of the store."

"This was called burglary when I went to police school," said Luke.

"Just keep looking the other way," Griff advised.

After they got off work protecting the store's property, they went to a steak house to eat.

"I'll have the rib eye, well done," Luke told the waitress, "and just green tea and water."

"I'd like the T-bone, coffee, and water, please," Griff said.

Griff turned to Luke and asked, "What did you think of what we saw this morning?"

"That really made me proud to be a Waukegan policeman," said Luke. "Those fucking cops are no better than the burglars we arrest at night. They're guilty of the same crime, but the ones we arrest go to jail."

"The whole system is like that here. Get used to it, improvise, adapt, overcome—remember that from your time in the Crotch? It starts at the top with the police chief and the judges. The mayor and city council know about it but look the other way. Don't even want to mention the sleazy lawyers. It's the same way there that it is here," concluded Griff.

"I don't want to be part of it—I'm going to be looking for a new job," said Luke. He cut his steak. "Umm, dead cow."

"I got a solid lead on a small town in northern Wisconsin that's looking for a new chief of police. I think I got enough time on the job to handle that," said Griff.

After the meal they left the restaurant. Griff said he was going to the range to do some shooting.

"I'm going to burn through a couple hundred rounds," said Griff.

"You still got that box of twelve gauge double-aught buckshot I gave you?"

"Yeah, but I won't have it when I leave the shooting range."

Luke was going to connect with Donna Gidoon again. He liked being with her.

Donna talked him into going to her office to meet the people she worked with.

As she was introducing him to the secretaries and paralegals, she announced to them that Luke was a patrolman in the police department. "One of the few good ones they have there," she added.

When he had met them all he asked if there was going to be a quiz on the names. They all laughed. He didn't meet any of the lawyers because they were in court defending people the cops had arrested.

Luke went to the police station to start his shift. He saw Griff inspecting the patrol car they would use that night. They were ready.

"This feels like getting ready to go on a patrol outside the wire," said Luke.

Their first call of the evening was for a car accident on the west side of town. Luke was wheeling through the traffic.

"You drive this car like a pro," said Griff.

"I wanted to be a race-car driver when I was a kid," answered Luke.

They arrived on the scene to find the two cars that had collided. Luke checked one for anyone with injuries, Griff checked the other. Then he walked back to the patrol car to call for a hook and a meat wagon. Three people in one car were a little banged up from bouncing around. In Luke's car the driver was complaining about chest pains.

They talked with the drivers of the two cars and got the information needed for their report. Both policemen had sniffed when they were close to the crashed cars—nope, no smell of alcohol or weed from either driver.

When the ambulance arrived the pair helped two of the victims to the wheeled stretchers. The paramedics began examining them, applying pressure bandages on the open wounds. Two ambulances left carrying all of the wounded.

The tow-truck driver called for a backup because they had two cars to haul to the lot.

Griff was filling out the accident report while Luke was taking pictures of the scene. He zoomed in for close-ups of the collision damage to the vehicles.

After the two tow trucks had cleared the wreckage, Luke and Griff continued patrolling. They got a radio call to meet the sergeant at an abandoned gas station. As soon as they arrived, the sergeant told them they were going to do a surprise weapons search at the Black Cat Tavern.

Four patrolmen came in the front door and stood there; four patrolmen were doing the same at the back door. The music was loud in the place, but one could hear the clunk, clunk sound of something hitting the floor. The patrolman in the front moved the people up against the wall in the rear of the bar. The patrolmen at the back door began shining their flashlights and collecting the guns and knives from the floor. Luke found a straight razor and one small .32 caliber revolver. The others who were searching found three knives and four more pistols.

The sergeant asked if anyone had a permit or owned any of the weapons piled on the pool table. No one stepped forward to claim any of the five pistols, so he put them in a bag he had carried into the bar.

"It's a slow night—we usually get more than five guns, three knives, and a straight razor when we do a raid like this. He threw the knives in the bag too. He thanked the crowd for their cooperation and the policemen left. They could hear the cuss words people were throwing at them: "Motherfucking pigs, dirty cops."

Griff walked out singing that song by Mr. Rogers: "It's a Beautiful Day in the Neighborhood."

After that it was an uneventful night for the two Marines riding in patrol car 603. They talked about women, ex-girlfriends, ex-wives, and muscle cars—Griff was a Mopar guy and Luke preferred a Chevy—also rapists and burglars and other criminals, corruption in the criminal justice system department, their time in the Marine Corps, and the broken Marines coming back from Vietnam.

That was their life, moments full of adrenaline and boredom in patrolling the streets.

"Six-oh-three, go to twelve forty-four Westchester, talk to the complainant there."

"Six-zero-three, ten-four."

"Six-oh-three, dispatch, we're ten-six at twelve forty-four Westchester."

Luke and Griff walked up to the house. It was a nice-looking house, painted white with black shutters on the windows. While walking up, both patrolmen looked around the well-kept yard, the driveway, and looked for damage to the house. They didn't know what they were walking into so they kept looking for information.

Luke didn't hear anything unusual as they approached the front door. Griff hit the doorbell; they listened as they heard someone approaching the door. A lock clicked and the door was opened from the inside. A white female invited them into the house.

"Good afternoon, ma'am, I'm Patrolman Griffith and this is my partner, Patrolman Warmwater. You wanted to speak to a policeman?"

"Yes. I'm Samantha Bellingham, and I wanted to talk to you about my son, Larry—Lawrence Bellingham. He's a junior at Savoy High School. He's at school now."

"What is it, what's the problem?" asked Luke.

"Just one minute, and I'll show you what the problem is." She stood up, walked out of the room, and returned with something clutched in her fingers.

It was a plastic sandwich bag that had some green plant material in it. She handed it to Griff. He looked at it, smelled it, handed it to Luke.

Luke looked at it and said, "Yes, this look like marijuana, looks like enough to make five or six cigarettes—joints, they're called. Where did you get this?"

"From under my son's mattress. I went in to change his sheets and when I pulled the bottom one out, this came with it."

"When does he get home from school?"

"In about five minutes," she replied. "Can you talk to him in such a way that he won't forget?"

"Sure, we can do that."

"Have you noticed any changes in him, any behavioral problems? asked Griff.

"No, Patrolman Griffith, he's his sweet, lovable self."

"We'll have a heart-to-heart with him when he gets home."

Soon, a tall, gangly boy came walking up the driveway. He looked at the police car all the way into the house. He opened the front door, kicked off his shoes, and said, "Hey, Mom, what are the police doing here?"

"They want to talk to you. I'll be upstairs."

"Have a seat, young man."

"I'm Patrolman Warmwater and this is my partner, Patrolman Griffith. What does your mom call you?"

"Larry. She calls me Larry."

Griff and Luke had worked together long enough that they took turns being good cop and bad cop.

"Will you tell me where you got this?" asked Griff, throwing the sandwich baggie on the coffee table. "Your mom said she found it under your mattress this morning."

"I've never seen that before in my life," answered Larry.

"Okay," Luke said, "Before we go any further, let me read him his Miranda rights.

"You have the right to remain silent as long as you can stand the pain," said Luke, leaning toward the boy and playing the bad cop.

"What do you mean?"

"We'll go easy on you as long as you answer the questions," answered Griff. He was smiling as the worried teenager looked at him. "I asked you where you got this marijuana."

"It's not mine, I was holding it for this guy in school, he's a senior. He said he got it from some Mexicans on the south side of town."

"What is this senior's name?"

"I can't tell you that—he'd kill me."

"I think it's his marijuana, let's take this lying sack of shit downtown and throw him in the cellblock," growled Luke, abruptly standing up.

"Wait a minute, wait. I'll tell you his name," said Larry.

"He's lying, just take him downtown so he can tell his story to the judge—Judge Rodriquez who hates drugs and druggies, since his daughter died of an overdose."

"His name's Jerry Ellis, he's on the football team."

"See, I knew he would cooperate with us," said Griff, slapping Larry lightly on the shoulder.

"Larry, run upstairs and get your mother."

Eager to get away from the two Waukegan policemen, Larry ran up the stairs, taking them two at a time.

He came back down, holding his mother's hand.

"Larry, I think it would be a good idea if you apologized for bringing that weed into her house."

"Mom, I am so sorry I got you involved in all of this—sorry for bringing the marijuana into the house."

"I think you should tell your dad about this whole thing too," said Griff.

"I will—I'll tell him right after he gets home tonight."

With that, the two patrolmen stood up, put their hats back on, and walked toward the front door.

"Thank you both, I didn't know who else to call."

"We'll be seeing you around, Larry," Luke said.

"No, you won't, Officer."

They walked back to their squad car, fired up the engine, and called dispatch.

"Six-zero-three is ten-eight."

"Six-oh-three, ten-four."

Griff looked at Luke and said, "Judge Rodriquez? There ain't nobody with that name on the bench.

"I know. Jorge Rodriquez was one of my fireteam leaders in India Company in the 'Nam."

"What should we do with the weed?" asked Griff. "If we turn it into the Narcotics Division they'll just flush it. This is small potatoes—they like to go after pounds and kilos of the stuff."

"You ever smoke that in the 'Nam?" asked Luke.

"Sure, did you?"

"That's a big yes, buddy. I used to smoke it before it got dark and watch those flares floating down all night. They looked so pretty, swinging back and forth; the way they would make the shadows move around, the squeaking noise they made swinging."

"I used to smoke it when we could get it. I thought it made me so careful, always on the alert for anything that could hurt me or my boys."

They continued on their journey through their memories and the streets and alleys of Waukegan.

As they were cruising down the street they saw a hippie-looking guy sitting on a bench—looked to be waiting for a bus.

"I know what to do with that marijuana," said Luke. "I used to do this all the time when I was a deputy; pull over by this guy."

"You want to talk to him?"

"Yeah, you'll see what I got in mind."

As the patrol car slowed in the street, Luke was rolling his window down. He was using his right hand to wave the hippie-looking guy over to the patrol car.

The man cautiously approached. "Yes, Officer?" he asked.

"Sir, would you do me a favor? Do you see that sewer grate behind you?"

"Yeah, I see it."

"Would you pour this sandwich bag down into the grate?"

"Sure, no problem."

Both Luke and Griff watched as the man accepted the sandwich bag, rolled it open, and poured the marijuana down into the sewer.

"Thank you, sir," Luke said as Griff wheeled back into the traffic lane.

"Do you think it broke his heart to pour that marijuana into the sewer?" asked Griff.

"He's probably cussing us out now. When he gets back to his crib no one will believe this just happened to him."

"You got a devious mind, Luke Warmwater."

"Yeah, I'm just as worse as you."

"I've been meaning to ask you, what was life on the Reservation like? What is there to do there?"

"Well, the hunting and fishing are good. We should plan a fishing trip up there."

"Do I need a passport or anything to get on the Reservation?"

"No, the Reservation was broken up seventy or eighty years ago, so now we own about a quarter of it. The rest is owned by white homesteaders, paper companies—even the University of Minnesota owns a big chunk of it."

"What about your chief? Do I have to let him know I'm up there on the tribe's land?"

"No, we don't have chiefs anymore. We have a form of government that's run by Roberts Rules of Order. We do have something a lot of places don't have, though. We have wild rice—*manoomin*, it is called—five good lakes on the Reservation. We control those lakes so we have a crop year after year."

"I heard about that wild rice. People say it tastes good and it's hard to find."

"We can probably pick up a couple of pounds while we're there. A lot of people still make rice every September. A lot of Indian people also make maple syrup."

"So, why'd you leave to come all the way to this hellhole called Waukegan?"

"No jobs on the Rez, and the white people got a pretty good lock on jobs that open up. There's racial discrimination. We don't have many black people living there so we take their place on the hit parade of racism."

"Let's take a trip up there in June. The fishing should be good then."

"Yeah, let's plan on doing that."

"On the Reservation, do they still use the language they used before the white man came?"

"Yeah, I don't know very much of it because I went to a boarding school when I was six, so my language learning stopped then. The old people's attitude was it was better for us to learn English, it would help us succeed when we grew up. The longer I stayed away from the Reservation the less I knew."

"Do you have a word for a cop?"

"Yeah—the one I know, my grandfather taught me: *gizh-adigewinini*. It really means 'game warden' because that was the only law around in the old days. Even learning that one helped when I was a deputy on the Reservation, or as we call it, the Rez. There are eleven Reservations in Minnesota; seven of them are my people, the Anishinaabe. The others are Dakota.

"Can you count to ten in your language?"

"Sure." Luke held up ten fingers and folded them down as he counted.

"*Bezhig, niizh, niswi, niiwin, naanan, ingodwaaswi, niizhwaaswi, ishwaaswi, zhaangaswi,* and *midaaswi.*"

"Let me hear you count to one hundred."

"Sure, but you'd get tired of hearing it and quit listening and think of what you want to say instead of listening to me."

"Okay, then, what are the words for twenty, thirty, forty, and fifty?"

"*Niizhtana, nisimidana, niimidana, naanimidana.*"

"The word *ashi* just means 'plus' and it's added between the words like this: the number twenty-one is *nizhtana ashi bezhig*, twenty-two is *niizhtana ashi niizh*. See the pattern? It is like that all the way up."

"This is really interesting, you Indians are more complex than I thought."

"Gee, thanks—or *mii gwech*. You white guys are more complex than I thought," chuckled Luke.

"Does it bother you that some of the other patrolmen call you 'chief'?"

"No, I heard that shit so much when I was in the Marine Corps it doesn't bother me at all. I like it that most of the night shift calls me by my name."

"Uh-oh—burnt-out headlight on that one car coming, let's take a closer look."

Luke swerved into a gas station, came around, and fell in behind the car. The people in the suspect car didn't even notice them until Luke turned on the red lights and gave a three-second blip on the siren.

They made a tactical stop; they looked at the suspect car like there was a keg of beer in the backseat, assorted firearms in the trunk, and the people inside were escaped convicts on their way to score some weed.

Luke and Griff were watching the two people in the car—they were especially watching for the shoulder slump: when trying to hide something under the seat, most people will slump their shoulder down.

Luke pulled in behind the suspect vehicle, got out of the car, and stood behind the front door. He could hear Griff open his door; Luke knew Griff was drawing his weapon but keeping it down by his leg.

Their spotlights were lighting up the interior of the car. Both approached the car and, after looking in the backseat, explained to the driver their reason for stopping them.

Luke was polite, he said, "Good evening, sir, license and registration, please. Oh, by the way, you have a headlight out."

As usual, Luke was standing a bit back, forcing the driver to turn in the seat to look at him. Griff had moved up so he could see in the rear seat, and from there he was watching the passenger.

The passenger slowly did the slump. Griff moved up, opened the car door, and invited him to step out, watching his hands the whole time. He took the passenger to the trunk and told him to lean forward and put his hands on it. Luke was doing the same thing to the driver.

When Luke was guarding the two suspects, Griff holstered his pistol and drew out his flashlight. He shined his light under the seat and saw the blue steel part of a weapon. He yelled loud enough for Luke to hear: "Gun."

Luke ordered the two suspects to raise their arms, lace their fingers behind their necks, drop to their knees, and cross their ankles. He stuck his foot between one suspect's feet so if he made a quick move Luke could pull backward, throwing the man down on his back. Griff came back, grabbed the laced fingers of one of the suspects, and while holding them together, did an upper-body pat down. Luke did the same with his suspect. Once they were cuffed they were put in the backseat of the patrol car. The backseat passenger doors didn't have door handles or window cranks on the inside.

Both patrolmen went forward to do a real search of the car. Griff pulled out the pistol that was under the front seat. Luke didn't see anything else suspicious there, so he grabbed the car keys and walked back to begin looking in the trunk. Griff was searching in the backseat. He found seven 12 gauge shotgun shells stuffed between the seats. He came around to help search the trunk just as Luke was lifting out an oily rag. He opened it and saw a pump shotgun. The barrel was cut off and when Luke pumped the slide back, a shotgun shell flew out of the weapon.

He picked it up and compared it to the ones Griff had found. They looked the same.

Luke called dispatch and asked for a record check on the name listed on the driver's license. Griff was interviewing the passenger; he asked for his name, then read both men the Miranda warning.

The record check came back, and the driver was identified as a fugitive with a bench warrant issued. The passenger was identified as an escapee from a neighboring county's jail. Luke called for a hook to come and tow the car the suspects had been driving.

Luke got on the radio and arranged for the detectives to meet them at the station.

The shift sergeant arrived and told the two patrolmen they would get credit for the felony arrests.

Luke and Griff got back on the road and talked about their credit for felony arrests.

There was no actual quota, but patrolmen were graded on how many moving violation tickets they wrote, how many parking tickets, and how many arrests—misdemeanor or felony.

The scores were tallied every month and the top two scorers had their eight-by-ten photographs hung in the police department lobby. Soon, Luke's and Griff's photos were hung: they were Patrolmen of the Month.

CHAPTER SIXTEEN

Luke's life was evenly divided between his duties as a patrolman and his time spent with Donna Gidoon. He was finding his niche as a cop and gladly becoming Donna's lover. His nightmares from the war were diminishing, he noticed.

After they had been dating for about six months Luke went to Donna's apartment. He thought she didn't sound good when he called to tell her he was coming over; she'd been lying on the couch when she got up to answer the door. Luke walked into the darkened apartment. The lights were off and the window shades were drawn. There was a blanket and bed pillow on the couch. She was wearing a blue terry-cloth robe.

"I get these terrible headaches and the bright lights make them worse," she said.

"Have you talked with a doctor about them?"

"I hate going to doctors. Their whole idea of medicine is, let's run some tests to keep you coming back. I've hated and avoided doctors since I was a little girl. One of them must have scared me."

"Do pain relievers help?"

"I tried different kinds, nothing works. The only thing that works is time," she replied.

"Well, if you keep getting headaches there's something wrong," he advised.

"Okay, if I get one more after this one ends I'll go to a doctor," she promised.

"How about if I rub your temples?"

"Let's try that. I like when you touch me in other places too."

Luke got the pillow and sat at one end of the couch. She slowly lay down and gingerly put her head on the pillow. Luke moved her hair and began lightly rubbing her temples.

After about twenty minutes she grabbed his fingers and said the pain was going away. Luke smiled, glad that he could help her.

"I usually get real tired when these things end."

"How about I leave for a while and come back later?"

"That would be nice," she said.

He called her about two hours later.

"Hello?" she answered.

"Hi, Donna. How are you feeling?"

"Rested and ready to spend some time with you," she replied.

"*Butch Cassidy and the Sundance Kid* is showing at that theater downtown. I can pick you up so we could see the one that starts at 1900—oops, I mean seven o'clock."

"You get the tickets and I'll get the popcorn," she replied.

"Okay, I'll pick you up about quarter to seven then."

Luke and Donna continued dating, growing closer as they shared good times. He casually asked about her headaches. She said she still got them, and only time and a darkened apartment and his fingertip massage took them away.

One afternoon when he picked her up from work she mentioned she had talked with her parents. They had asked about her headaches, and when she said they still bothered her, were more frequent, her mom suggested she come home to Indiana to see a specialist. In fact, she'd already made the appointment.

"I'll be leaving next Sunday, should be gone for a week or so," she told Luke.

"I can drive you down there," Luke offered.

"It's about a six-hour drive there. You can meet my folks, I've been telling them about you for a while now. And Mom was hinting that she wanted to meet you."

"How does she feel about Indians?" Luke asked.

"She said she had never met one. She didn't have any feelings one way or the other. She had a lot of questions, but the most important one was how you treated me."

"Simple, I treat you like I would like to be treated."

"That's one of the reasons I like you."

"I only have two days off but I can take a vacation day or two," Luke said.

"Okay, I can show you around town, show you where I graduated from high school, where I used to hang around with my girlfriends."

"I've never been to Indianapolis, but I know they have the Indy 500 there every year. Okay with you if we drive my car? It's bigger and you can stretch out more.

"But before we go there I want to stop in Chicago for a visit with my sister Doris. She lives near Broadway and Lawrence on the North Side. Doris said she wants to meet you. You've met all of my other sisters, but not her."

The sun woke them up on the first day of their trip. They ate a big breakfast of scrambled eggs, oatmeal, fried potatoes, and toast. He did the cooking and she did the dishes.

They loaded their car with the suitcases and rode the freeway to the North Side of Chicago. He didn't know much about the streets, but he knew enough to drive directly to Broadway and Lawrence. He liked going there because there was family at the end of the journey.

On the way Luke told Donna an old family story. It seems Luke's grandfather Joe was selected to accompany some old chiefs to Washington, D.C.—this must have been in the early 1900s. Joe went along as an interpreter because most of the chiefs didn't speak English. The Anishinaabeg had time to look around while waiting for the next train. They were so amazed at looking at all of the tall buildings that Joe said the roofs of their mouths got sunburned. He tilted his head back to illustrate how they were looking at buildings every time he told that story.

Doris lived on the third floor of a huge apartment building. She was between boyfriends when they came to visit.

She was still holding on to her job in a factory. Her job was to help assemble something. When Luke asked what she made she didn't remember. Her job was tedious but it paid the rent and the rest of her bills.

He wanted Donna Gidoon to like her as much as he did. He was pretty sure they would get along.

Doris made some coffee as they sat around the kitchen table. While visiting she had time to get up and make fry bread. She mixed the dough while the oil was heating. The smell of fry bread filled the kitchen. Luke said it triggered many memories of life on the Rez.

It didn't take long before Doris set a platter of tasty fry bread on the table. All of them began eating. Donna hadn't had it before so she asked Doris for the recipe. Luke hadn't had fry bread in so long he ate three pieces of the fluffy, good-tasting bread.

"Doris, when was the last time you had wild rice?"

"Two nights ago. When I was home last time, Gramma stuffed my suitcase when I was leaving. I was wondering why it was so heavy when I dragged it through the bus station. She must have put eight or ten pounds in there. I'll give you a pound to take home."

"Good for you—you always were her favorite."

"That's because I always helped her, whether she was cleaning or baking or picking food from her garden."

Doris and Donna were getting along well. They really liked each other. Doris was promising that she would come up to Waukegan by train and visit them.

Doris was stroking her huge cat named Dog, and she began to talk about him. She said in her last apartment she was on the third floor. The pigeons used to land on her windowsill and coo and coo her to sleep. Dog didn't like pigeons cooing and shitting on his windowsill. He would jump up to the windowsill, scaring the pigeons. After a while the birds saw that the screen kept the cat on his side of the window.

One day Dog couldn't take it anymore and jumped through the screen. He began falling. He stretched out and rode the air down to the ground. When Doris checked where he landed it was between the sidewalk and the building where the ground was soft. She found four paw prints and one long belly print where the cat landed. The pigeons never did come back.

Luke and Donna decided to get back on the road. Before they left, Doris sat them back down and said she wanted to tell Donna a story about Luke.

Doris said, "I was living over there on Third Avenue—big place and I had the ground floor.

"One day Luke stopped by for a quick visit. He brought this woman with him, they were attending a conference or class or something.

"All I'm going to say about her was she wasn't pretty.

"We had a nice little lunch and then Luke and that woman had to leave to get back. I waited until she was in the car and called Luke back to where I was standing on the porch. He came bouncing up the stairs and stopped at the top.

"I walked over to where he was, and with a flick of my wrist I popped the bag open. It was a brown paper grocery sack. I handed it to him and told him it was just in case he got lucky later that night."

She turned to Donna and said, "I'm not going to give him a sack this time. Instead, I'm giving you this bag of wild *manoomin*. Cook it like regular white rice, surprise your mom and dad with it.

They really didn't want to leave, but Donna had an appointment the next day with her old family doctor.

They cruised through the expressways of Chicago and took I-65 heading south to Indianapolis. Luke was driving and Donna was telling him about Doris.

"It feels like all of your sisters are my sisters too. I'm an only child but your sisters make me feel like one of them. I just wish I could tell a story like Doris."

"She has that knack for storytelling. A common trait of the Anishinaabe who lived on the Rez before electricity came to the little village."

The interstate signs were blipping by as they rolled down the smooth highway toward Indianapolis. Luke saw cornfields. He told Donna, "When I was six I ran away from Pipestone Boarding School. I was captured by two mean white men in a cornfield like this."

She looked at the cornfield and tried to picture a six-year-old Luke running away.

Donna explained life in the city here, she said the whites mostly lived on the north side of town. Her parents lived in a suburban condo complex, which had tennis courts, an indoor pool, an outdoor pool, and party rooms.

Luke was impressed with the decor. It sure was different from the way most of the people in Waukegan lived. He couldn't even compare it to life on the Rez. Weather and electricity were about the only things they had in common.

Shirley opened the door and stepped back and invited them in. Luke was carrying Donna's bag. Shirley was blonde and pale;

she dressed well in a summery skirt and blouse. She shook hands with Luke and looked deep into his eyes. She hugged her daughter. David came in from the den carrying a newspaper he had been reading. He shook hands with Luke and hugged his daughter.

The welcome-home meal was catered in the party room. Luke ate what was called finger food. He also had a watercress salad. He was offered wine but he politely put his fingers over the top of his glass and shook his head when someone attempted to fill it. As the meal party went on the wine was beginning to do its work and people talked louder. The music was louder too.

People were laughing and dancing. Every once in a while someone would come walking up to talk to Shirley and David. They talked to them but were looking at Luke.

He laughed to himself as if they expected him to sprout feathers or erupt in war paint on his face. He smiled. He had been at white people's gatherings a time or two, he had been stared at before. Luke didn't dance but just sat there smiling, not adding feathers or paint. He was practicing his stoic look all evening in the party room. He was glad when the party was over, the people were wobbling or wandering off.

Luke and Donna, Shirley and David walked back to the condo. The two old ones noticed the young ones were holding hands as they walked.

The four people sat at the kitchen table and talked over cups of tea. The old ones could see Luke and Donna enjoyed being a couple, laughing at the same time, eye-smiling at each other.

The conversation was about plans, and David came right out and asked Luke if they had ever talked about marriage.

"I want to go to law school first," replied Donna.

"I don't like being a Waukegan patrolman," Luke said. "I want to have a more secure profession before I consider a family."

"But we want grandchildren," Shirley said.

"I know you do, but first things first, as you always used to tell me," said Donna.

"Let me ask you, Luke," said David, "do you have a savings account?"

"Yes I do, and Donna and I have a joint account," answered Luke.

"Come on, David, it's time to turn in," said Shirley. To the young couple she said, "Don't stay up too late. Donna has an appointment at ten thirty with the family doctor."

Both couples went to bed. Luke and Donna were twined together all night long.

During breakfast Donna asked Luke, "Will you have enough time to drive home and get to work on time?"

"I added an hour of dumb time and I'll still get home four hours early," he assured her. "Will you call me after you see the doctor?"

"I will. Mom will be with me when I go in for the physical and probably tests."

"Good, I'll drive careful so I can see you again."

The drive home to Waukegan seemed to take longer than the drive the other way. Luke felt like he was leaving something behind—a part of his heart perhaps?

He arrived at his empty apartment and got ready for work.

CHAPTER SEVENTEEN

When he put on his gun belt, ankle holster, badge, and name-plate he became The Law. He returned to police work. He and Griff caught more burglars, arrested more felons, broke up more fights, and investigated more accidents than anyone else on the night shift.

They were righteous busts too—the guilty people went to jail, the innocent stayed free of the system.

"I got an interview next week, the mayor and police chief of Lily Pad Lake, Wisconsin, want to talk to me," said Griff.

"They're coming all this way to interview you?" asked Luke.

"No, they're going to a seminar in Chicago on how to get more LBJ poverty money. We'll meet when they pass by Waukegan."

"Did these two up-north guys bring their wives?"

"Yes, I'm going to meet them at the golf course clubhouse for dinner next Tuesday. I should know something one way or the other by the end of the night. C'mon, let's get going, those people aren't going to arrest themselves."

"Yup, they need us for that part."

"How was your trip south?"

"Donna went to her family doctor and he referred her to a specialist who called for a series of tests."

"In other words no news is bad news?"

"Something like that."

"I think you're going to run up a big phone bill. Long-distance love is expensive."

"We've got a joint savings account so we've been putting money in there and leaving it alone. I'll use that money for the phone calls if I have to. We had already planned for this."

The radio interrupted them. "Six-oh-three, shots fired near Twelfth and Stowe."

"Six-zero-three, ten-four, dispatch."

Luke hit the red lights and siren. Talk was difficult over the noise of the siren and radio. Other squad cars were checking in with dispatch letting everyone know they were on their way.

"What's at the corner of Twelfth and Stowe?" Luke asked.

"There's that all-night gas station called Crescent's on one corner, Johnson's Scrap Yard on the other."

"Okay, okay, I remember it now. That's near where we got that stolen car, remember? Did that guy really piss his pants when you stuck your pistol in his ear?"

"Yeah, that was the time."

Luke slid to a stop in the gas station driveway. They saw the attendant lying half-in and half-out of the front door. He wasn't moving. Luke went to check on him.

Griff covered him as Luke checked for a pulse on the attendant's wrist. Nothing, no pulse, Luke pointed at the shotgun lying on the pavement. There was a bullet hole in the front door, another larger hole in the plate glass window. There was no one else around.

Other squads began arriving. They set up a perimeter around the gas station. The detectives arrived and took over the investigation.

Luke and Griff returned to their squad car, and Griff began writing the report about what they did at the scene of the apparent robbery and murder. The ambulance arrived. The medical examiner also. He walked up to the body, cut open the attendant's shirt. Luke could see the jagged hole that was the exit wound. It didn't take long for the medical examiner to peel off his rubber gloves and pronounce the man dead.

"Does that poor stiff lying there remind you of the 'Nam?" asked Griff.

"Yeah, and the smell of the gunpowder added to it too."

"Let's get out of here before the detectives have us knocking on doors looking for witnesses."

"Yeah, they don't really need us here anymore."

The two Marines fought crime all night. In the morning Luke went home to wait for the promised phone call from Donna. He prepared a breakfast of oatmeal, fried eggs and potatoes, bacon and toast. While he was washing dishes the phone rang.

"Hello?"

"Hi, Luke." He recognized Donna's voice.

"How are you feeling?" Luke asked.

"I saw the specialist, he wants to do more tests. I may be here for a while—longer than we thought anyway."

"Did he give you any idea of what it was?"

"Yes, he said it may be a tumor, or perhaps brain cancer. They'll do a biopsy next. Oh, they're here for me now. I'll be wheeled in grand style down to where they do the injections so they can see on the X-rays. I'll call you at the usual time again."

"I care about you, Donna,"

"Me too, you."

"I'll be here at home waiting for your call."

Luke prepared his uniform for work that evening. He shined his shoes, cleaned his guns and ammunition. He ironed his shirt and trousers. He liked looking sharp as a Waukegan patrolman.

"How is that Donna girl?" Griff asked toward the end of the next shift.

"We're right in the middle of an unknown," answered Luke.

"What are the doctors doing with her?"

"Right now looks like X-rays and a biopsy. After that I don't know."

"Sounds like the doctors don't either, I hope she pulls out of it okay."

"Thanks, I hope so too. I'm wired, I think I'll go for a run in the state park."

"I'm going shopping for a new suit. I want to wear it for my interview with the police chief and mayor from Lily Pad Lake," said Griff. "I know the mayor was a Marine—that came up during the phone interview."

"I keep thinking about that dead guy at the gas station," confessed Luke.

"Me too."

"We've seen dead bodies before, but it seems somehow different to see them here at home."

"I know."

"But like in the 'Nam, all I can say is fuck it, and drive on."

"Better him than me," added Griff.

"Good luck with the mayor and police chief."

"I'll be polite and charming," Griff promised.

Luke was getting ready for his run at the state park when he suddenly felt heavy, like he could barely lift his feet. He sat down on the couch, then lay back. He fell asleep and the dreams began. This time, they were just fragments of dreams, some he recognized as having been dreamt before.

The sound was mortars being fired, whump, whump. Luke knew there were at least two rounds coming in to explode somewhere in

the Marine's perimeter. He also heard the sharper crack of hand grenades detonating.

Now it was bullets snapping by his head. Because of the sounds of the firefight Luke couldn't hear where they were shooting from. The sharp-sounding explosions reminded him he was in a war zone and could get hurt. He could hear the sound of a man screaming somewhere. He hoped it wasn't anyone he knew. He hoped it wasn't him. He didn't know what to do next.

He did know what to do, he was a Marine. He ran to the perimeter where the shooting was loudest. He could see people moving around outside the barbed wire. Those were enemy soldiers. They were shooting and moving.

Luke was aiming and shooting.

When Luke got off work the next morning, he went home and waited for the call. It was a phone call that would make him happy, or a phone call that would make him sad. It was out of his control.

The phone rang, an ice chill coursed through Luke. He picked up the phone and said, "Hello?"

"Luke? It's Shirley Gidoon with some very bad news. Early this morning Donna slipped into a coma and died."

"No. I'm very sad to hear that. When is the funeral? I'd like to say my goodbyes to her."

Luke knew even before she said anything that Donna was dead. He had been feeling something missing inside since the last flashback. Griff had tried to cheer him up by telling some raunchy jokes he had heard in the bar recently; the jokes didn't work. Luke hadn't answered with a chuckle, just answered with a look, and a slight shake of his head.

Griff sensed his mood and knew enough to leave him alone.

Luke packed a bag for a trip down south where Donna Gidoon was waiting for a funeral: her own. Her mother and a couple of ladies from the church made preparations. The funeral home had been notified as had the caterer. The minister from the church was writing his speech. The florist was happy with the calls coming in for flowers. The doctors were somber but were happy that their diagnosis was correct.

Luke sat in the rear of the fancy funeral hall. The plush surroundings were a sharp contrast to the death of a twenty-four-year-old woman. Luke shook hands and locked eyes with the friends and relatives of dead Donna. It was a long train of people that he grieved with.

Luke really wanted to get drunk, but he didn't because he didn't want to disturb the other mourners. His mouth watered when he imagined slamming down a shot of good whiskey. He could almost feel the little fire the whiskey started in his stomach. There was time to find a shot after the minister got done praising Donna.

Luke didn't want to grieve with these white strangers. He would leave right after the funeral feast.

On the long drive through Indiana, Luke was thinking of many things, but they all centered on the thoughts of death. Mr. Death, as Luke called him. Was he being paid back for the death and destruction he was involved in during his time in Vietnam? He remembered the old saying: payback was a motherfucker.

In his case he was realizing the results of payback. Two of the women he thought he was going to share his life with were dead in a little over two years. Was this the luck of the Irish? Wait a minute—I ain't Irish, I am Anishinaabe, thought Luke. But Anishinaabe have bad luck too. We're all human and we all have joys and sadness.

He stopped for coffee and tried to cry but couldn't.

He headed back to Waukegan. Of course he had to stop and tell Doris the news when he got to Chicago.

Luke found a parking spot right in front of her apartment building. He rang her doorbell. He waited a bit then heard her walking to open the door. As soon as she opened it she knew something was wrong.

"Where's that Donna girl? I want to see her again."

Luke's eyes told her all she needed to know.

Doris screamed and began crying right away. She hugged Luke and said, "Not Donna girl."

Luke shook his head yes, and held on to Doris. She kept saying, "No, no, not Donna."

"It was brain cancer and she went quickly," Luke explained. "I went to the funeral but I had to leave that gathering of white people. I was the only one there who had dark skin. One young girl complimented me on my tan. Let's go to the liquor store. I want to drink my pain away," finished Luke.

"I'll go, I'll get a case of beer. And do you still like that single malt scotch?"

"Yeah, it's called Glenfiddich and it goes down smooth."

The brother and sister drank all their beer and whiskey that evening. The next morning Luke thought he was sober enough to drive so he made a run to the liquor store—the jug store, he called it.

Once again they drank all of the beer and wine they had purchased. The alcohol did what it was supposed to and both of them were asleep before the ten o'clock news even started on TV.

The next morning Luke told his sister he had to get home to go to work. She said they were lucky their days off happened at the same time.

Luke got back to his house and prepared for work. He shined his shoes and ironed his shirt and trousers. The last thing he did was clean his two pistols: the one on his hip and the one in the ankle holster. As he finished and was wiping them with a light oil, he was hoping he wouldn't have to use them tonight.

CHAPTER EIGHTEEN

Luke buried himself in police work; it was the only thing he had going in his life. He thought he would wait a long time before getting involved with another woman. He nodded to Griff when they assembled in the briefing room.

"Well, how was the funeral?" asked Griff.

"It was as good as any funeral could be," answered Luke.

"You've survived the deaths of your friends, mines, and many clicks of humping through rice paddies—you'll survive this too."

"Yeah, let's go get some bad guys. I know they've been waiting for me to get back."

As the night went on Griff observed that Luke was the more aggressive of the two of them. Where he was ready to give people a warning, Luke was happy to take them to jail. During one foot chase after a fleeing suspect, Luke outran Griff to grab the bad guy and had him cuffed before Griff caught up.

"Who died and made you Super Cop?"

"I just got a different attitude about things. If I'm arresting bad guys then I'm doing something right for the world."

"Do what you gotta do, just don't get me killed. My mother would be so pissed about that."

Luke and Griff stopped to eat at a coffee shop. It was 0200 and most of the drunks had gone home.

"Are you going to Sergeant O'Brien's retirement party? asked Griff.

"I don't think so."

"Aw, c'mon, we can hang out with the guys who were in Vietnam."

"Yeah, okay, I'll go."

"I heard O'Brien's giving away a plum part-time job."

"I'm looking for something to do on my evenings off—they are pretty empty now. I'll talk to him about it. What's the job?"

"It's that savings and loan place on Ninth Street. You just guard the place during the evenings. You don't have to wear a uniform because your post is in an empty office that overlooks the interior of the association building. A 12 gauge shotgun is the weapon of choice for that job. You just watch everyone that comes inside; they can't see you because of the two-way mirror there."

"Sounds interesting, I used to like carrying a shotgun on ambushes. Like a rifle shot means I'm talking to you, a shotgun means I'm talking to all you all," said Luke.

"Not too many guys have Fridays off, so you got a good chance he'll give it to you."

"I'll talk to him, tell him how much I like shooting people with a shotgun."

"Don't act too crazy—he isn't real sure about the guys who've been in Vietnam."

"Okay, I'll cool my jets and talk like a model citizen."

After they finished their shift and slept awhile, Griff and Luke went to the party at a fancy hotel downtown. The upper ranks in the police department were thanking Sergeant O'Brien for his years of service, his dedication to the blah blah and also his blah blah blah. The mayor made a token appearance and shook the sergeant's hand. The photographers were firing flash bulbs at the festivities.

When the speeches were done the gathered policemen settled down to some serious drinking and storytelling.

Luke went to where Sergeant O'Brien was sitting and congratulated him on his long career. The sergeant had heard of Luke and was happy to see he wasn't drinking alcohol, that instead he was sipping tea.

Luke came right out and asked, "Sergeant O'Brien, I heard about your job for the savings and loan association on Ninth Street. Will you keep working there now that you're retiring?"

"Nope, I'm hanging up my badge and gun. Hey, I noticed you're drinking tea."

"That's right. I don't like how booze affects me. I think I know it all and sometimes get belligerent and say stupid stuff."

"I've been on the wagon for a bit over ten years myself, water only. Before I quit drinking I lost a wife, a daughter, and almost lost my job on the police force. You interested in that Friday evening job at Midwest Savings and Loan?"

"Yes, I am."

"You're the fourth person to ask me about it but I think you'd be the best one to work for them. I'll call Dennis Peterson and let him know you're my choice."

"*Mii gwech*, I mean, thank you."

At this point in the party the Vietnam vets moved away from those who hadn't served. They gathered in tight little groups to tell stories about their time in the war.

Griff explained things to Luke about these storytelling sessions. "Do you know the difference between stories and war stories?"

"No, what's the difference?" asked Luke.

"A regular story starts off with 'Once upon a time.' A war story starts off with 'This is no shit.'"

"Well, I hope to hear some 'This is no shit' stories tonight."

After listening to the stories Luke decided to tell one of his own. He grinned because he knew he hadn't told Griff this story during the many hours they spent in squad car number 603.

"This is no shit, it happened to me. Do you know that old French fort by Marble Mountain? We spent a week there one time. We were waiting for supplies and some replacements."

"I had the afternoon off so I decided to be a tourist. Everyone else I invited to come with me just wanted to lie around the fort. We had just spent two hard weeks sloshing through the rice paddies.

"I wanted to climb one of those mountains to see what I could see, maybe take some pictures. On the first one east of Highway One was one that had steps going up the side. I walked through that little village to get there. I wasn't expecting trouble but wasn't foolish. I had my M14, a hundred rounds of ammo, four frags, and my Ka-Bar. I climbed up there, walked around the top, and took pictures of the South China Sea. I also took pictures of the little village that was near the mountains.

"I found a cave that had a bigger-than-life-size statue of the Buddha inside. Buddha had both arms in the air, the palms of his hands were facing in. I looked closer and it looked like Buddha was giving everyone the finger. Both hands. Then I could see where someone had broken off all the fingers except the middle ones.

"I looked around the cave a little bit and found some empty C-ration cans. I wondered if other Marines had been there.

"Some time later I found out the caves in Marble Mountain contained an NVA hospital. I wondered if the bad guys knew I was there."

"I can picture myself doing dumb shit like that too," added Griff.

"Me too," added Taylor.

"I think the chillingest, shortest story I heard came from a corpsman," said Griff. "He was working on the hospital ship and had heard it from a Marine. The recon Marine said, 'A patrol went up the mountain, one man returned, he died before he could tell us what happened.'"

There was a long period of respectful silence after that story.

"Damn, that is a spooky story," someone said.

Griff told a story about their enemies, the Vietcong.

"My platoon captured a couple of them after overrunning their trench line near An Hoa. In doing that they had killed all the other members of the Vietcong squad. These two were seriously wounded. One had been shot through the stomach and the top of the knee—that bullet had entered and traveled along the leg bone, splitting and laying the calf muscle open. The other VC had been shot through the head and neck. Big chunks of both parts were missing. The VC were minutes away from dying. There really wasn't anything we could do for them, they would have died before we got a medevac chopper in. The corpsman came over and gave each a shot of morphine. He didn't want them in pain as they died. Isn't it strange to sit around watching and waiting for someone to die? Two someones?" said Griff.

"Didja ever see how Charlie modified a single-shot M14 to be an automatic rifle? They'd use a ball-point pen spring and a grenade pin in place of the selector switch. It worked just like the original, changing back and forth. They had three M14s like that. They wounded a couple of Marines with those captured weapons. Payback is …," was all he said in finishing his story.

The retirement party continued even though Sergeant O'Brien had gone home. It was an hour or so after the good sergeant left that Luke decided to go home too.

◇◇

A few days later, Luke went to work at his usual time after squaring away his uniform and cleaning his pistols. He met Griff in the roll-call room and they walked out together to check the patrol car. After that, they hit the streets.

Squad car 603 was dispatched from one calamity to another well into the night. After the bars closed the calls got farther apart.

Griff and Luke had plenty of catching up to do. Griff said his meeting with the mayor and police chief went well. He expected to leave Waukegan to work as the police chief in Lily Pad Lake in northern Wisconsin. He would be putting two hundred miles between himself and the corruption in the Waukegan Police Department.

With this news Luke felt like he was losing a left arm.

"If you have any openings you could hire me away from Waukegan," Luke told his partner.

"You'd get first dibs on any opening that comes up," he promised Luke.

◇◇◇

Feeling that police work would not be the same for him now, Luke decided to see if the public defender needed an investigator with five years of street experience.

Luke arranged a meeting.

They met in an upscale restaurant called the Porterhouse. Luke and Donna had eaten there twice before, and the wait staff remembered Luke. He was known as a good tipper. Luke arrived early and as he was being led to his seat, he picked the booth they would use. From there Luke could see the front door and the entire room. It was that old survival trick he had learned in Vietnam.

Bill Wilson came walking in right on time, his eyes sweeping the crowd. He nodded to the owner of the Porterhouse. He walked up to Luke and introduced himself and said he wanted to get to know him. He looked slightly overweight and had a small bald spot—a hole in his haircut as the Indians say. He smiled easily.

As they ate together Luke was being measured by Wilson; the seemingly innocuous questions continued throughout the meal. Luke knew he was being grilled by an expert. He just answered the questions as truthfully as he could.

They talked about the current war in Vietnam, about Luke's service there. Bill shared that his older brother was a Marine and how much he admired him. He also wanted to know about life on the Reservation in Minnesota.

They talked about combat, about court, about the law. Bill asked Luke about some of the exciting cases he had worked on. Over dessert Bill asked about Luke's family.

Luke said, "I'm single, never been married. I came close a couple of times."

"What happened to the close ones?"

"The first two died of poisoning, the third wouldn't eat the sandwich I made her."

"Are you serious?"

"No, that was a joke."

"Okay, I get it, a sense of humor is important in the criminal defense system. What happened really?"

"Carrie died when a logging truck pushed her into a stand of pine, the second one just died of brain cancer. She was Abbey Donna Gidoon, and she worked in your office.

"I knew she'd been dating a cop. We were all devastated when she died, she was so young. Donna was the best paralegal we ever had."

"I knew she was good at her job. In her memory I decided to ask you for a job—a chance to continue working in the field she loved. I knew you were looking for an investigator."

"You'd leave the police department to work on defending the people you used to arrest?"

"Yeah, it was too crooked there. By wearing the same uniform as them, I was condoning what they were doing. I worked the night shift and I dreaded going to work every afternoon."

"I'll tell you right now, we have a problem here in the office. Every year for the six that I've been here, the budget goes down. Our caseload goes up but the money to represent the poor goes down. It gets hard to attract good lawyers. The best we can do is try to grab the sharp ones from the graduating classes of the law schools. One old criminal defense lawyer told me that good criminal defense attorneys were either dead before age fifty-five or were drunks."

"What happened to the last investigator you had here?"

"Nothing, we have never had one. The grant Donna was working on was funded so we have money to hire an investigator. I don't know if we can replace Donna Gidoon, however. In all of my ten years of law practice she was the best I ever worked with."

"Yeah, she was quite the human being," Luke agreed. "I miss her very much—and probably will for a long time."

"Any questions for me about the position?" asked the public defender.

"Yes—what are the duties?"

"At first you'll interview all of the new clients we get as they come in. If you feel the client isn't being entirely truthful we want to know that right away. You had five years working with people on the street, so I'm sure you developed a good bullshit detector. After you get the feel of the place here, there will be other duties as assigned—perhaps tracking down witnesses, reviewing police procedure, photographing crime scenes. I'll introduce you to the attorneys and support staff, although I did hear that you already visited once. We have staff meetings on Mondays, Wednesdays, and Fridays, usually in the afternoons."

Bill continued, "So what do you think? Are you up for the challenge?"

"When can I start?" responded Luke.

"How much notice are you going to want to give the police department?"

"Ideally, three weeks, but I can start in two. What are they going to do? Fire me?"

"I like that attitude, I think you'll fit in fine at our office. We'll take a tour if you have time this afternoon. You can meet whoever's not in court."

The law office was located in an office building, but the bottom floor was for businesses. One of them was a bar named the Gavel, a lawyers' hangout. Luke wondered if a bar was necessary for the practice of law. The building was a block away from the courthouse.

Both men entered the elevator for the short ride upstairs. There was a large sign that said Public Defender, Second Floor. Some wag had added with marker: "There ain't no more."

A chime sounded when they walked into the office. The room was painted institutional green and had bookcases along most walls; the shelves contained law books. There was a large electric clock on one wall. Three women were at work with typewriters and file folders.

Bill Wilson introduced Luke as their new investigator to Sarah, Janet, and Shirley. They had last names, and Luke would learn them as time went on. He shook hands with them and they returned to work.

Bill and Luke walked down the hall to an office.

"This is John Milston's office, he mostly handles felonies," said Bill. Luke saw a short man, maybe about five feet seven. He had blond hair, blue eyes, and a beard.

"John, this is Luke Warmwater, our new investigator," said Bill.

They shook hands and Luke noted it was a firm grip. They looked at each other's eyes.

"I heard a bit about you from some of the older cops. You were called 'Chief Lockemup' behind your back," said John.

"I never heard that. I would have unfucked it if I had."

Both lawyers smiled, they looked at each other and nodded.

"I do mostly felonies, but we all cover for each other because no attorney, no matter how good, can be in two places at once."

The pair walked over to the next office.

"This is Susan Goldberg's office," said Bill. "She does mostly felony cases but helps out with the misdemeanors." Turning to the lawyer, Bill continued, "Susan, I'd like you to meet Luke Warmwater, our new investigator, formerly with the Waukegan Police Department. He also worked on his Reservation as a deputy sheriff."

Luke shook hands with Susan. She had blonde hair and dark brown eyes, about five feet six, and dressed in a conservative suit. A single strand of pearls adorned her neck. There was a slight aroma of flowers coming from her.

"I'm glad to meet you, Susan," said Luke, "I guess we'll be working on some cases together. Now, let's see if I got this straight right from the start. You're the attorney and make the decisions. I help by getting the information you need to make decisions for your clients."

"That sounds good to me," she said. "I'm looking forward to sharing information with you. My door is always open and so is my mind."

They left her office and walked down the hall.

"This will be your office," announced Bill.

Inside, Luke could see a desk and a file cabinet. He sat down at the swivel chair and opened one of the drawers. Inside he found a thirty-five millimeter camera; it was a single-lens reflex. Luke was familiar with these because he owned a similar one. In a smaller case Luke found a flash attachment. He also found a stack of legal pads and pens, pencils, and other office supplies. The file cabinet was empty but contained a package of folders. He noticed the door had a mirror on the back. There was a calendar on the wall and on the desk pad. An electric clock was over the doorway. The large window provided a view of downtown Waukegan.

"Next door is the bathroom," said Bill. "On the other side of that is Peter Winslow. He handles mostly misdemeanors. Right now, he's in court with his clients.

"Andrew Cunningham is the last attorney you'll meet that works here. He's also in court with his clients. He has a mix of felonies and misdemeanors. The door after that leads to my office, and after that is the conference room. That's where we have our staff meetings."

"I'm sure I'll learn everyone's name once I start seeing them every day," Luke said.

"Right," said Bill. "Now, our first order of business when you get back from your final week with the Waukegan Police Department will be to order some business cards and make you an ID card so you can get into and out of the various jails in the area. By the way, I'm curious: what will your fellow policemen say about your abrupt decision to work here?"

"I think most of them won't care one way or the other. I'll miss hanging out with the veterans from Vietnam, though."

"We'll be getting some people in to work as interns and paralegals in a couple of weeks when school starts. Perhaps you can work with some of them too."

"Okay. I'll check in with you when I'm done being a patrolman."

"Fine, fine. Don't get yourself killed during these last few weeks. I hope you won't dread coming to work here. If you do, come and see me so we can talk about it."

◇◇◇

Luke reported for work and wondered who he'd be riding with on his last nights as a Waukegan policeman. He'd quit his part-time job in the bank and passed it on to Taylor, another veteran.

He saw that he was assigned to ride with Tolliver, a black veteran of the Vietnam War who had served his time as a grunt. Tolliver was driving, Luke was writing the reports of their activities. About a half hour after they started patrolling they got a radio call.

"Six-oh-three."

"Six-zero-three, we're at the nine hundred block of Twelfth Avenue South."

"Six-oh-three, motor vehicle accident at Nineteenth and Wilson Street."

"Six-zero-three, ten-four."

Tolliver drove to the intersection of Nineteenth and Wilson. They looked around, no sign of an accident—nothing unusual going on.

Tolliver called it in. "Six-oh-three, dispatch, nothing here, no signs of an accident."

"Six-oh-three, the accident is at Ninth and Wilson."

"Six-zero-three. Ninth and Wilson, ten-four."

"Goddamn it, they sent us to the wrong intersection. I hate it when the dispatcher makes mistakes like that," said Tolliver. "What if someone is in the crashed car, bleeding? This just pisses me off."

With that, Tolliver threw the car into reverse and backed up rapidly to turn around. The squad car hit a light pole, which stopped them right away. Luke's head hit the headrest, his hat flew into the shelf under the rear window. Tolliver's head hit the headrest then bounced forward into the steering wheel, which cut a large gash in his forehead.

Luke recovered from the crash and grabbed the first aid kit and put a compress on Tolliver's cut. He picked the radio microphone off the dashboard.

"Six-zero-three, dispatch."

"Go ahead, six-oh-three."

"There is a motor vehicle accident at Nineteenth and Wilson. It's us. We need a hook and a meat wagon at this location."

"Six-oh-three, ten-four, rolling a hook and a meat wagon."

"Six-zero-three, ten-four."

A sergeant supervisor arrived first. The fire department arrived because the sergeant noticed the gas tank was leaking. Both patrolmen were standing outside looking at the damage to their car and the pole; Tolliver was still holding the bandage on his face. The car taillights were looking at each other and the trunk had popped open, though the pole was undamaged other than some paint peeled off.

"Who was driving?" asked the sergeant, while looking at the cut on Tolliver's face.

"I was—didn't even see that pole," answered Tolliver.

"You'll have to make out an accident report when you're done at the hospital. I'll have to make one out too."

"I was in a hurry to get to that accident at Ninth and Wilson," said Tolliver.

"I know, I heard the whole exchange on the radio. The dispatcher's going to have some explaining to do," promised the sergeant.

"Did you get another squad to answer the original call?"

"Yeah. Six-oh-seven is at the scene. Doesn't sound too serious."

The ambulance arrived and both patrolmen got in for the ride to the hospital. Tolliver was placed on the stretcher and Luke sat with him. He was rubbing his neck, where he felt a huge cramp.

They got to the hospital and Luke was taken for X-rays while Tolliver was being stitched up. Luke's X-rays came back; the doctor said there was no serious damage to his neck. He'd be sore for a couple of days but should recover nicely. Tolliver had eight stitches for the cut. Luke waited while Tolliver went in for

X-rays. He came out and the sergeant drove them back to the station where their private vehicles were parked; earlier, he had driven to the tow yard and picked up their property from the wrecked squad car.

Luke drove to his place and got into the shower right away. The warm water beating on his neck took most of the soreness away. Luke stayed in there for quite awhile. He wanted to tell Donna about the accident, then remembered she was dead.

When they reported to work the following night both were given light duty and were assigned to work around the station. The other patrolmen were calling Tolliver "Crash." Crash went to work with the dispatchers and Luke was sent to the detective division, where he met the detectives again. He knew a couple of them, had stayed with them for two weeks learning how they worked, their policies and procedures, their gossip, their hates.

◇◇◇

Luke told his friends in the police department he was leaving to work for the public defender. For the most part, the patrolmen and detectives respected his decision.

Luke's friends gave him a small party, though no one over the rank of sergeant attended. The evening was full of cop stories, toasting, and drinking. When someone suggested moving the party to a strip club, Luke went home. He had turned in all of the Waukegan Police Department equipment, including his ID card and badge. He was finally free of that corrupt setting, he could face that guy in the mirror again.

PART THREE

CHAPTER NINETEEN

He wondered what adventures were waiting for him at the public defender's office.

Luke had a few free days before he was supposed to check in, so he drove south to Chicago to see his sister Doris. He wanted to tell someone about the car crash.

They became tourists and Doris taught him about riding the El; the rattling noisy trains carried them around the city. They went to the lake—the waters of Lake Michigan were a different color from the lakes back home. The green color looked unusual to the two *Shinnobs*. They went to the Loop, Wrigley Field, and the airport. In the time they spent together they talked fondly about the people and life back on the Rez. Both were homesick but wouldn't admit it. They talked about making syrup, making wild rice every year. They also missed the funerals and dances. They talked about moving back home, how easy it would be to return and be part of the community again. That was it, Luke thought, he didn't feel a part of anything in the big city.

Luke thought about his little apartment in Waukegan and told Doris he was going back to his place. Doris planned to come and visit him: she could just jump on the train and be in Waukegan in less than forty-five minutes. She wanted to see where he spent his time.

Luke found the garage where he had parked his car a couple of days before. He drove north thinking about his new position as investigator; he also thought about his two dead loves. He decided that he would not get involved with anyone for a long time. He wondered if Mr. Death were still following him as he traveled through life. Luke thought of many things as he drove.

Monday morning he walked into his new office, greeted the secretaries and researchers, and got a cup of coffee. He went down the hall to his office. He boldly walked in, sat in his swivel chair, and looked around. Luke decided that he needed something on the walls. Maybe pictures of his family, pictures of the Rez. He didn't want to put any pictures up from the war. That sore hadn't scabbed over yet.

He noticed a file with a note attached. "Read me first," it said. The note was signed by John Milston. The half-inch-thick file was a murder case.

Luke sipped his coffee and read the file. The defendant was named Alvin Savage; he shrugged slightly when he read the name. "Alvin Savage" was something that Alvin Savage would have to overcome, especially the "Savage" part. A murder suspect named Savage?

Alvin Savage was a veteran of the fighting in Vietnam and was charged with shooting his girlfriend, Jasmine Wilson. Both were black—victim and suspect. In the back of the file was a set of photographs supplied to the defense team by the Waukegan Police. Luke looked at the photographs of the murder victim. She had been shot in the stomach and had two wounds in her head, entry and exit. The bullet in her stomach had apparently hit an artery because there was a large pool of blood under her. Luke went back to the police report. He read the one written by the first officers to arrive at the scene. He read the detectives' reports and the autopsy. He read all of the police reports.

When he was finished, he called John Milston and told him he'd finished reading the file. John suggested they meet downstairs in the Gavel to eat lunch and talk about the defense.

Luke had a cheeseburger, the specialty of the house. He had a tall glass of ice water with his meal. He remembered all the times when he had to drink rice-paddy water when the helicopters couldn't come in to resupply the troops.

John Milston had the cheeseburger too. He washed his down with a bottle of imported beer. When they were done eating John began talking about the Savage case.

"I'd like to hear your thoughts on the case," John said.

"I wish our client had a different last name."

"Yeah, I thought that as soon as I picked up the file for the first time."

"From reading the police reports I think the police officers did their jobs correctly. Alvin was given the Miranda warning before they asked the first question, and I see they sent Alvin's rifle to the ballistics experts but didn't see their report."

"Well, now that you mention it, I didn't either. Under the rules of discovery we're entitled to that piece of information. I'll call the prosecutor to find out what the delay is. I'm glad you caught that—I was so busy preparing for the grand jury hearing I had forgotten about the ballistics report."

"Did the client talk with the police?" Luke asked.

"No, every time they tried to question him he refused to answer their questions. He just lowered his head and shook it back and forth."

"Did you warn him about talking to anyone about his case? The police have been known to put a snitch in jail to dig for information."

"Yeah, I did," the attorney said. "That was one of the first things I told him. Now, I'd like you to go to the jail and talk with him, introduce yourself as the new member of his defense team."

"Sure—I'll go over there after we're done here. I've never worked on a murder case before."

"Don't worry. Remember what I said about a defense team? Right now it's just you and me, but we'll be adding expert witnesses to our team—you know, fingerprint and polygraph examiners, our ballistics people, maybe a psychiatrist or two. The theory of the defense in this case is yes, he did shoot her, but he's not guilty based on a mental disease or defect. It's an uphill struggle, but we'll do the best we can with what we got. Alvin's a veteran of the Vietnam rice paddies like you."

◇◇

After their lunch Luke picked up his ID card from one of the secretaries. He slipped the card into his wallet and told her he would be at the county jail. She also gave him a pager in case someone had to get in touch with him right away.

As he walked to the jail he thought back: not too long ago he wore a cartridge belt that held a hundred rounds of 7.62 ammo, he had a bandolier with sixty more rounds, a twelve-pound rifle, two quart canteens, four frag grenades, a flak jacket with curved fiberglass plates, and a steel helmet. Then as a cop he had a leather gun belt that held his service revolver, six rounds in a reserve speedloader, a nightstick, and, if he was lucky, a handheld radio—also a pair of handcuffs. Today he carried a pen, a notebook, and a pager. He was moving up in the world as his load went down.

When he got to the jail he showed his ID card as he signed in. The jailer recognized him right away.

"Hey, Chief Lockemup, you jumped ship—you're working for the enemy, those defense lawyers. We'll have to give you a new name now. How about Chief Unlockem?"

"Fuck that 'chief' shit, I wasn't in the U.S. Navy. How about just plain Luke. Call me Luke and I'll call you the name your momma gave you. What was it?"

"My mom called me Elmer, I was named after one of my uncles."

"Okay, Elmer, buzz me through. I'm here to meet one of our clients."

"Who is it?"

"Savage, Alvin Savage." The jailer smiled when he heard the name.

Luke walked into the lawyers' room. Inside he found a table with two chairs facing each other. Luke noted the table and chairs were bolted to the floor. He sat and waited.

The deputy jailer brought in his prisoner. He was a black man, about six feet one or so, 220 pounds. Alvin Savage wore handcuffs attached to a belly chain. He had black hair and brown eyes; he was wearing a jail uniform of gray coveralls, white socks, and cheap slippers.

"Ahh, Deputy, can you remove the cuffs and belly chain until we're done talking?"

"Okay, but if something happens it'll be your fault."

"We're just going to be talking about legal matters and his case," Luke said.

"Okay." The deputy unlocked the handcuffs, pulled the belly chain off his prisoner, and left the room.

"Hi, Alvin, I'm Luke Warmwater," he began. "I'm an investigator, and I'll be working with John Milston as part of your defense team. Your guilt or innocence in this case doesn't matter to me. I make sure the attorney has all of the information he needs to defend you. Got any questions for me?"

"Yeah, when were you in the 'Nam? You have that look and your eyes say that you were there. I was with the One Seventy-Third, an Eleven Bravo."

"I was there early, sixty-five to sixty-six. I was an Oh Three Eleven, a Ninth Marines grunt."

"That was some shit, eh?"

"Sure was. I saw things I'll never forget."

It was quiet in the room while both veterans were remembering.

Luke started, "Once we were set up on this hill south of Da Nang. It had been a long day and the choppers couldn't come in because of the weather, so no resupply of food and water. We had plenty of ammo—boocoo ammo. The captain said we'd be meeting trucks in the morning so we didn't have that long hump back to the combat base. We'd run the VC off that hill, got a couple of wounded there. So we set up for the night, and for some reason we had an extra sixty with us and some eighty-ones. We started getting fire from that little village at the base of the hill. We answered back with the guns and the tubes. After the mortars quit firing we could hear a baby crying in the dark night. There was nothing we could do—would have got shot up trying to move around in the dark, so we stayed in place and just listened to that baby cry. The baby cried for about an hour, then he finally got tired or died and we didn't hear him anymore. Then on the other end of the village another baby started to cry. That one went on and on and cried until almost daylight. To this day I can't stand to hear a baby cry."

"Yeah, me too, had something similar happen, crying babies," said Alvin, looking at the floor while shaking his head. "It's such a helpless feeling knowing babies were crying and dying around you and you couldn't do anything."

Then he said, "Were you where a lot of guys smoked weed?" asked Alvin.

"Yeah, almost everyone smoked at one time or the other," replied Luke. "The senior sergeants didn't but almost all the snuffies did. Could get a Salem cigarette pack full of rolled joints for two hundred piastres—a little less than two bucks. It was potent stuff too. One guy couldn't smoke a whole joint. The Motor T drivers used to deliver it by the sandbag. Trade them an empty sandbag for a full one. I forgot what we paid for that. I know guys were trading captured weapons too. The rear-echelon pogues really went for captured weapons—everyone wanted an AK-Forty-Seven. We could roll big joints using the pages from a

Bible when we didn't have rolling papers. We started at the Old Testament."

After a pause, Luke said, "The music on the box sounded so much better when I was stoned, I remember." said Luke.

The two veterans talked about their experiences in the war for an hour.

Finally, Luke said, "Want to talk about your case? I read all the police reports. I'd like to hear about it in your own words."

"It's kind of hard to talk about, but I feel like I can trust you."

"Do you mind if I take notes as we talk?" asked Luke.

"No," replied Alvin. Then, "Jasmine was a beautiful woman, she said she loved me and wanted to spend the rest of her life with me. We were living together but something was wrong, I could feel it. She just had to see this guy she used to go with, the things she said didn't add up. The last straw was when she came home smelling like him. I just couldn't take it anymore."

"What happened then?"

"I followed her to his place, waited for her to come out. When she did I shot her in the stomach, didn't want to mess up her face for the funeral. She went down but I could tell she was still alive so I walked up, shot her in the head. Then I put the rifle down and sat there and cried. I was still sitting there when the police arrived—one took my rifle and the other handcuffed me. I thought they were going to shoot me. I wanted them to shoot me."

"That's some heavy shit, man," said Luke. He pictured the whole thing happening, the loud boom of the rifle, the surprise on the victim's face, the coppery smell of blood.

"You're the first person I ever told about my side of the shooting. I hope you don't think I'm crazy."

"No, I don't think you're crazy."

"I just want to plead guilty and go to prison," said Alvin.

"Don't give up. If we can convince one juror that your time in combat affected you like this, we got a chance for a not-guilty verdict. This is without a doubt a new and unusual legal tactic. Let's talk with your attorney before you decide to plead guilty."

"Now that I told you what happened, I feel relieved. Now that is some crazy shit," said Alvin. "Isn't that weird?"

"No, it's not. You're not carrying it by yourself anymore. Okay, Alvin, I'm going back to talk with your attorney," finished Luke.

◇◇

When Luke left the jail he felt like he needed a stiff drink. The images were flooding his brain. He called his sister Doris but she wasn't home. Instead of a stiff drink, he had a tall glass of ice water.

Luke exited the jail and walked back to the office to talk with John Milston while the conversation was still fresh in his mind.

He called John and was invited to his office. He brought the file with him, also a blank legal pad. He got another tall glass of ice water. He was ready for the debriefing.

Luke walked down the hall to John's office and rapped politely on the doorframe.

He heard, "Come in," so he did.

Sitting in one of the visitor's chair was a distinguished-looking white man—about fifty years old, wearing a pinstripe suit and highly polished wing-tip shoes. His looks and demeanor screamed "professor."

"I'd like you to meet Doctor Nathan Whelan, who'll be assisting in our case," said John.

Luke shook hands with the doctor; his grip was warm and strong. After a few seconds both sat down and faced John.

"How did the initial visit with our client go?" asked John.

"We had a good talk—I spent about two hours with him," answered Luke. "He's a grunt, an infantryman."

"What topics did you cover?"

"He asked if I was a veteran. I told him I was, and we shared some war stories before we talked briefly about the crime he's been charged with. He wanted the responding police to shoot him, and now he just wants to plead guilty."

"That sounds like deep remorse to me," said Doctor Whelan. "He's feeling sorry for what happened. I'd like to meet with him, talk with him, and maybe administer some tests."

John faced the doctor and said, "I'll arrange the time and place for you at the jail."

"Have you worked with combat veterans before?" asked Luke.

"I have. I just retired from working at the VA hospital in North Chicago and I've had many counseling sessions with veterans from the Korean War. I've never worked on a case like this, however."

John said, "Basically, what we're trying to do is convince the jury that Alvin Savage is not guilty of second degree murder, because he was insane at the time of the shooting. This insanity lasted only a short time and he began acting normal after a few hours."

He continued, "Sandy Johnson, a paralegal, will be working with me too. She'll prepare and file the necessary motions as we begin building the case. She'll come and talk to you both when she needs to.

"Luke—I'll need crime scene photos, diagrams, and a neighborhood canvass to find witnesses the police may have overlooked."

"Okay," said Luke, "I can do that. By the way," he continued, "I noticed we still haven't received the ballistics report yet."

"I'll call the prosecutor about that again," said John.

Luke left the office and took pictures of the crime scene, including some from the shooter's point of view. He drew several diagrams, then he canvassed the neighborhood. He found two witnesses the police hadn't talked to, but they'd only heard the shots and hadn't actually seen anything. One man reported seeing Alvin Savage sitting on the ground crying after he heard the shots.

The Friday staff meeting included attorneys John Milston and Susan Goldberg, Dr. Nathan Whelan, paralegal Sandy Johnson, and Luke. A woman arrived from the administration section; she was there to take notes of the proceedings.

John started off by welcoming everyone to the defense team. He asked Dr. Whelan to report his findings.

"I had a couple of intensive interviews and administered several tests. I believe Mr. Savage was insane when he shot Jasmine Wilson. The tests and interview notes are included in my report—I see you all have copies."

Sandy Johnson was next; she reported on the motions she had filed.

Luke's photographs and diagrams of the crime scene were passed out to all members of the team. The notes from his interviews of the potential witnesses were also included in his report, and there was, finally, the ballistics report from the prosecutor's office.

John Milston addressed the group. "Fine, fine. We're all moving along here. Now, there is one more thing I want you to remember as we continue working on this case. Not only are we defending Alvin Savage, we are also defending the Constitution of the United States."

With that, the meeting ended.

Before John left, he called Luke back and handed him another file. "It's another murder case," he said.

"Thanks, John. I'll prepare my part of the case: photographs, diagrams, and witness interviews. He looked at the name on the top of the folder. "I'll go see her right now," he said.

Luke set up an interview with Carol McDonald, a forty-five-year-old white woman who was charged with murder for shooting her husband, Kenneth McDonald, while he slept in his recliner. This was Milston's case, with Goldberg sitting as second chair. Luke went to his office and read the file.

Luke walked to the jail so he could talk with the woman who had shot her husband six times. She hit him once in the face, twice in the chest, twice in the stomach, and once in the groin. Luke cringed when he read the autopsy report; the crime scene photographs were especially grisly. There were no witness statements. The gun, a .357 Magnum Ruger, was found on the coffee table by the first officers on the scene. All of that information was included in the police reports.

He waited while the deputy brought Carol McDonald into the interview room. She was wearing handcuffs and a belly chain. The deputy asked if Luke wanted them removed. Thinking that it would improve communications, Luke nodded yes—it had worked with Alvin Savage.

She was about five seven, maybe 150 pounds, had short blonde hair and blue eyes. Her skin was pale white and she looked like a housewife who was wearing oversized jail coveralls.

Luke introduced himself. "Hi, Carol, I'm Luke Warmwater. I work with Attorneys Milston and Goldberg. I have just a few questions I'd like to ask you."

"I'll try to answer them, this is all so strange to me," she began. "This is the first time I've ever been arrested," said Carol.

"Okay. Can you describe the events of the afternoon after your husband came home from work?" He opened his notebook.

There was a long period of silence, lasting a bit over three minutes, before she began to speak. As Luke waited, he noticed Carol was sitting in a way that could only be described as rigid.

After a sigh, she began to speak, softly at first, then getting loud-er as she went on. She was getting more animated as the words came tumbling out.

"He came in. Kenny slapped me when I told him I didn't pick up the beer and whiskey yet. He said he was going to take a nap and if the drinks weren't there when he woke up, he would slap me again."

"Was that common? Your medical record shows numerous visits to the emergency room."

She was now waving her arms around and even pounding on the table with a fist. "Yes, Kenneth had a nasty temper—it got worse when he was having problems at work or when he was drinking. He broke my arm once, several ribs too, when he punched me. I felt like Kenny's punching bag. I had to get stitches four times when he hurt me. We also had a miscarriage because of him. I knew where he kept his bullets and gun."

"Go on," encouraged Luke.

"I loaded the pistol— Kenny taught me how to do that. He was showing me how to defend myself when he was gone from the house. I walked into the living room, I could hear him snoring in his favorite chair. I listened to his sleeping noises for a long time, then he started stirring like he was going to wake up. I got scared and raised the pistol and shot him in the side of his head. I kept shooting until the pistol just clicked."

Luke noticed she was shivering, even though it was seventy degrees in the jail. Tears came to her eyes.

Luke didn't ask any more questions; he let the silence calm both of them down.

He left to go back to his office.

The two murder cases were weighing on his mind as he walked. The files he had read, the conversations he had had—they were wearing deeply on Luke. And his conversation with Alvin Savage had triggered some terrible memories.

◇◇

He remembered Da Nang Air Base.

He was lying facedown in a water-filled ditch after the Vietcong 122 millimeter rockets began coming in and exploding. He lay in the ditch with nothing to shoot at as the explosions happened around him. He would never forget the particular whistling noise they made.

It was louder than a mortar round but not as loud as an artillery shell impacting and exploding. Luke was picturing a rocket coming down and hitting him in the middle of his back. Would he feel it hit? He feared the rockets.

◇◇

Luke was hoping to make it past his ninety-day probation period, but the cost of helping other people when they were trouble was too much.

He couldn't take the pain. He wondered why he was wallowing in the sewer of humanity.

He called Doris in Chicago and told her how he was feeling. She listened and offered some thoughts and suggestions.

He met with the public defender. Apologizing, Luke said he couldn't do the job.

He thought some more and decided.

Fuck it, I'm going home.

For more tales of Luke Warmwater,
read on for an excerpt from
Walking the Rez Road.

Available now at fulcrum-books.com

FRITZ AND BUTCH

"No shit, it was the vice president of the United States."

"Sure it was. And I suppose he brought the pope with him," said Dunkin Black Kettle.

"No, it was just him. He had all kinds of Secret Service guys with him," said Luke Warmwater. "See, I even got his autograph," he said as he handed his cousin a piece of paper with a signature scrawled on it.

"Yah, right. Anyone can write like this. You can't even make out what it says."

"It says Walter F. Mondale. See, right there. It's his name, right there in front of you, in black-and-white."

"Give me another piece of paper like this and I'll make you another autograph. What name do you want me to scribble?" asked Dunkin.

"Watch the TV news tonight. See if they talk about the vice president visiting Duluth today."

Luke and Dunkin were in the bar at the Radisson Hotel. A housing conference was being held there. Luke joined the Indians who were celebrating the end of the day's business.

Dunkin was making his moves on three women from White Earth Reservation. He'd called his cousin to come and help snag the three women. He'd also called another cousin, Butch Storyteller, to come join them.

As usual, Butch was late, so Dunkin and Luke were doing their best to entertain the three out-of-town visitors. Just as Dunkin was getting started on one of his best stories, a Secret Service guy came in the bar, gave it a professional once over, and stood by the door.

The Indians were curious now. "See, I told you," said Luke as the Indians watched to see what was going to happen. Walter Mondale and his entourage walked by the entrance to the bar and proceeded to the elevator.

"I'll be damned. I caught you telling the truth," said Dunkin as he resumed his snagging. He wasn't getting very far because the conversation kept returning to the subject of the vice president.

Since they were talking about the vice president instead of vice, like Dunkin wanted, he put his snagging moves on hold. He figured he could use the vice president's visit to his advantage. The Indians drifted out to the hall to catch a glimpse of the vice president when he came back down in the elevator.

"I wonder if Butch got lost. He was supposed to be here a half hour ago," muttered Dunkin as he watched the White Earth women wander off.

"How could he get lost? He's lived around Dull Tooth all his life," answered Luke.

"He'd better get here pretty soon, or there'll be no reason to come down here."

"Ding," said the elevator as it opened and disgorged four Secret Service guys. They fanned out and checked the hall for possible danger.

The Indians were all lined up along one wall, sipping their drinks, waiting for Fritz to make his appearance. The Secret Service was lined up on the other side of the hall, watching the Indians and the rest of the crowd gathering. The Indians talked, joked, and laughed as they waited.

About this time, the local TV crews arrived and set up their lights and cameras. They were going to tape the vice president as he walked by.

"I'll get his autograph for you," Dunkin told one of the White Earth women, as he resumed his snagging moves.

"Ding," said the elevator. The TV lights came on, the crowd collectively leaned forward, the Secret Service tensed up. All eyes were on the door, waiting for it to open.

The door opened, and Butch came strolling out. He was whistling a nameless tune. The lust in his eyes was replaced by fright as he saw the lights and all the people standing there looking at him. He was dressed in a Levi's jacket and was wearing a bone choker on his neck. The Indians recognized him right away. They were laughing and applauding.

"Speech, speech! Can you comment on your policy on Indian housing, Mr. Vice President?" the Indians asked Butch. Butch walked out about four steps, froze, then spun around and tried to get back in the elevator. He was there to snag, not meet the media or be escorted by the Secret Service. The doors closed in his face. He tried to pry them open with his fingers, but that didn't work. He faced the doors for a long three seconds and then finally turned around.

He recovered his composure and, in his best Richard Nixon impression ever, threw his arms in the air, made two peace signs with his fingers, shook his jowls, and said, "My fellow Americans." The TV lights were turned off.

"Ding," the elevator doors opened again and Fritz came out. He looked slightly confused as he saw the Indians gathered around Butch, laughing.

The TV lights came on again and Fritz walked through the crowd, shaking hands and smiling. He was also signing autographs. Dunkin went up to Fritz and got his signature on a piece of paper. It was the same piece of paper Luke had showed him earlier. Fritz smiled as he recognized his signature. He signed it again and gave it back to Dunkin.

"Anybody can get an autograph, I got you two of them," Dunkin told the White Earth woman. She put the paper in her purse, and they all went back to the bar. The White Earth women and the Fond du Lac men sat down and began to get to know each other.

"Let me tell you about the time the three of us jumped on a plane and went to a party in Wisconsin," said Dunkin as he gazed deep into the eyes of the woman he was sitting with.

"This isn't the first time this has happened to me. I think Fritz kind of looks like me," Butch told the woman he was sitting with.

Luke smiled. Life was back to normal.

About the Author

Credit: Zsuzsanna Rozsa

Jim Northrup is an award-winning journalist, poet, and playwright. He is a combat Vietnam veteran serving with India Company, 3rd Battalion, 9th Marines, 3rd Marine Division in-country from September of 1965 until September of 1966.

His syndicated column, *Fond du Lac Follies*, was named Best Column at the 1999 Native American Journalists Association convention, and he holds an honorary doctorate of letters from Fond du Lac Tribal and Community College. His previous books include *Rez Salute: The Real Healer Dealer*, which received Honorable Mention from the 2013 Northeastern Minnesota Book Awards, and *Walking the Rez Road: Stories*, winner of the Midwest Book Achievement Award, Minnesota Book Award, and Northeastern Minnesota Book Award. He lives in Sawyer, MN.